Will the newlyweds ever have perfect peace?

"People say nothing is perfect, but I don't think it can get much better than this." Damon's voice turned husky and he kissed her waiting lips. "Home first, so we can change to jeans and sweatshirts?"

"Right." Arm through his, Nancy walked happily beside him. "Isn't it nice that some of the days we'll remember most aren't holidays or special days?" She felt him tense and glanced up at him. Every trace of gladness had fled. Damon looked as if he had fallen from heaven to utter torment in the space between heartbeats.

"Damon?"

Strong, protecting arms whirled her toward him and pressed her face hard against his chest. "Dear God, when will it end?"

His ragged voice cut into Nancy like a knife. What didn't he want her to see? She was a nurse, wasn't she? She tore free and turned, expecting a gruesome accident, wondering why there were no sirens.

No accident marred her view, but something far more ugly. Nancy swallowed hard to overcome nausea. Damon's late model white Toyota waited in the consulting doctors' reserved parking lot, as it always did when he visited Shepherd of Love. Except all four tires had been slashed.

COLLEEN L. REECE is one of the most popular authors of inspirational romance. With over 100 books in print, including twenty **Heartsong Presents** titles, Colleen's army of fans continues to grow. She loves to travel and at the same time do research for her historical romances. Colleen resides in Washington State.

Books by Colleen L. Reece

Books under the pen name Connie Loraine

Glowing Embers

Colleen L. Reece

Heartsong Presents

A note from the Author:
I love to hear from my readers! You may correspond with me by writing:

Colleen L. Reece
Author Relations
P.O. Box 719
Uhrichsville, OH 44683

ISBN 1-57748-149-6

GLOWING EMBERS

Cover illustration by Brian Bowman.

PRINTED IN THE U S A

prologue

For a single moment, she saw his face—etched against the lurid light of flickering flames.

She never forgot.

❧

Twenty years later, she saw his face again—outlined against a sun-glorified, stained-glass window.

She never forgot.

❧

Nancy Galbraith, RN and Dr. Damon Barton stood in the late autumn glow of a sun-glorified, stained-glass window that turned them to living mosaics. Free at last of the memory of searing, flickering flames, they pledged themselves to one another in sickness and in health, for better and for worse. For a single moment, heaven touched earth, brighter with promise than the sun-sparked ripples on the dancing blue waters of Puget Sound.

For a single moment.

one

Thy word is a lamp unto my feet, and a light unto my path.
(Psalm 119:105)

A graceful brown finger traced the Scripture neatly engraved on Seattle's Shepherd of Love hospital director's door. A warm smile curved Nancy Galbraith Barton's tender lips, lighting candles in her dark eyes. Her immaculate peach uniform lent a glow to her brown-velvet skin.

"How many times have I stood in this spot?" Nancy murmured. Her thoughts trooped on. How many times had she and other hospital personnel reverently touched the motto Nicholas Fairchild chose when led by God to create a hospital that combined Christianity and medical skills—a hospital open to all, regardless of the ability to pay; a hospital operated by finances generated only by making its needs known to God, then allowing Him to supply, usually by touching the hearts of those in a position to contribute generously.

Seattle civic leaders had predicted the hospital would never be built. Nancy's laugh rang out like the soft chime of silver bells, breaking the silence of the corridor. She moved her hand from the engraved words to the soft green walls. What a perfect background for the murals depicting mountains, woods, and streams. When white stone walls, sun-mellowed to a warm cream first graced a hill overlooking Puget Sound on one side, Mount Rainier on the other, scoffers labeled it a fluke. They also maintained it could not stay open more than a few months.

"That was years ago," Nancy whispered, mind still busy with the past. Shepherd of Love, named for the One Nicholas knew as the real hospital founder and director, continued to thrive. Wonder at its unorthodox practices continued, but any doubt about the quality of care given there had died long ago. Shepherd of Love was soon firmly established among the many other highly-respected Seattle hospitals. All of the institutions worked together to provide some of the finest medical service in the world.

A rush of happiness and gratitude brought diamond drops to Nancy's eyes. She passionately wished she could capture the moment and hold it close. Six months of marriage with Dr. Damon Barton, Children's Specialist, had proved joyous beyond her wildest expectations, yet such fleeting moments as this were rare and treasured. Nancy closed her eyes, feeling peace encompass her.

It wasn't always so, her heart reminded. A recent satanic plan to take over the hospital and oust the director had started with a single spark of treachery that kindled and came perilously close to succeeding. Chills swept through Nancy's shapely five-foot, eight-inch frame, leaving her weak. She sagged against the wall, feeling cold sweat crawl inside her collar.

A soft hand touched Nancy's arm. An even softer voice asked, "Nancy, are you all right?"

She straightened and turned. Tiny yellow-clad Shina (pronounced *Sheena*) Ito, Japanese American and the delight of Obstetrics, surveyed her with puckered brow, her dark eyes concerned. "Yes. I was just thinking what a privilege it is to be part of Shepherd of Love." Nancy's shaking hand crept back to the inscription. "And that nothing must ever be allowed to spoil it." Her insides churned, as if a glowing ember from a long-dead blaze had sprung to terrifying, threatening life.

"God won't allow it," Shina comforted. "He has prom-ised no weapon forged against those who serve Him will prevail." (Isaiah 54:17, NIV, paraphrased)

She looked solemn. "We just have to be eternally vigilant."

"I know." Nancy grabbed for the reins of self-control and

managed a wobbly smile. "Thanks for the little sermon."

"Any time," Shina replied, but a strange look crossed her attractive face. She hesitated. Nancy felt her longtime friend wanted to say more, but the smaller nurse shrugged, then asked, "What are you doing loitering outside the director's office, anyway? Waiting for your true love?" She didn't give Nancy a chance to reply but clasped her hands under her chin and donned a fatuous expression. "Be still, my heart."

"If your heart is located up there, you're in trouble," Nancy retorted, glad for the teasing that drove away unaccustomed dark thoughts. "With that knowledge of anatomy, your getting through nurses' training is. . ."

"Appalling," Shina filled in. "Now that I am properly chastised and set in the corner, what's up?"

"I really am waiting for Damon," Nancy said. "My car's in for service and it's such a glorious spring afternoon we plan to go house hunting."

"Really? Patti and I can be your first guests." Her eyes twinkled with fun.

"Sure, only don't expect steak or lobster." Nancy grimaced. "With the prices of houses, you'll be lucky to get spaghetti."

"Suits me fine. Can I bring a boyfriend?"

"If he likes spaghetti. Do you have someone in mind?"

Shina smiled tormentingly. "Maybe." She expertly changed the subject, but not before Nancy's keen eyes caught the same fleeting expression she'd seen earlier.

"Have you seen any houses you like?"

"We thought we had." The corners of Nancy's mouth turned down. "Until the last storm sent them hurtling down a cliff toward the Sound! Believe me, we are not buying anything on a hill unless there's a ten mile plateau on top."

Damon stepped into the hall. Nancy's heartbeat skipped to staccato. Had it only been a year since she met the tall, athletically-built doctor with springy black hair and dark eyes that held both compassion and sadness?

"What a faithful wife, waiting for her husband while he loiters," Damon praised. He draped an arm over Nancy's shoulders and kissed her cheek. "Hi, Shina."

"I just made reservations for Patti and me at Barton Manor," she announced.

"Are you still taking my name in vain?" a laughing voice demanded as blonde Patti Thompson joined them.

"Talk about a trick question! That's as bad as the one, 'Have you stopped beating your wife; please answer yes or no,'" Shina objected. "When I was doing you a favor, too. I could have just asked if I could be Nancy and Damon's first guest, but oh, no. I included you. This is the thanks I get?"

"Sorry." Patti's blue eyes rounded with innocence but she didn't look penitent. "Are you really buying a house? What kind? Where? When?"

"We'll tell you when we know." Damon threw his head back and laughed, a contagious sound that snuggled into Nancy's heart like a kitten in a welcoming lap. Her lips curved in an answering smile. She cherished laughter. It helped heal the long-ago loss of mother and sister against a backdrop of flames.

At the end of the corridor, Nancy and Damon turned toward an outside exit and the parking lot. Shina and Patti headed for the dining room, voices fading in the distance. "It's good to have Patti more like her old self," Nancy commented.

"Right." Damon smiled in the way that always made his wife's pulse accelerate. "Finding out someone you care for and trust is unworthy is always shattering." He sobered. "We are so blessed, Nancy." A poignant light shone in his dark eyes. "I hope someday Patti and Shina will have marriages like ours."

"So do I," she told him, then fell silent while they walked past spring-green lawns broken by golden beds of daffodils and colorful tulips. She longed to share what she had felt earlier. Reserved not so much by nature as by years of being on her own, Nancy often found it hard to express her deepest feelings even to the husband she adored. Now she searched for words. "Damon, do you experience times so special it actually hurts because you know you can't hold on to them?" Her heart thumped with longing for him to understand.

"Once in a great while." Damon paused and looked at her majesty Mount Rainier, the snow-covered monarch that kept watch over the hospital and city.

"That's how I felt today while I was waiting for you," Nancy whispered. She leaned against him and let her gaze follow his. An eagle floated against the sky. A spring breeze shook branches on the spruce, fir, hemlock, and pine trees that were so much a part of the hospital grounds.

"Do you think we will ever be happier than we are at this moment?"

Damon tightened his hold and she heard the steady beating of his heart.

"I don't see how. I didn't think I could ever love you more than on our wedding day." Nancy spoke so low he had to bend his head to hear her. "It doesn't compare with what I feel now."

"I know. People say nothing is perfect, but I don't think it can get much better than this." Damon's voice turned husky and he kissed her waiting lips. "Home first, so we can change to jeans and sweatshirts?"

"Right." Arm through his, Nancy walked happily beside him. "Isn't it nice that some of the days we'll remember most aren't holidays or special days?" She felt him tense and glanced up at him. Every trace of gladness had fled. Damon looked as if he had fallen from heaven to utter torment in the space between heartbeats.

"Damon?"

Strong, protecting arms whirled her toward him and pressed her face hard against his chest. "Dear God, when will it end?"

His ragged voice cut into Nancy like a knife. What didn't he want her to see? She was a nurse, wasn't she? She tore free and turned, expecting a gruesome accident, wondering why there were no sirens.

No accident marred her view, but something far more ugly. Nancy swallowed hard to overcome nausea. Damon's late model white Toyota waited in the consulting doctors' reserved parking lot, as it always did when he visited Shepherd of Love. Except all four tires had been slashed.

The vandalism barely registered in Nancy's stunned brain. Only the word *NIGGER,* spray painted in blood-red and repeated a half-dozen times.

A station wagon pulled into the lot. An intern leapt out. "What's going on?" He glared at the car, then turned to Damon and Nancy, looking as sick as she felt. "How could such a thing happen, here of all places? I'll call the police." He sprinted off as if pursued by Satan's full army of angels.

"Why did it have to be on our perfect day?" Nancy demanded brokenly, but Damon didn't reply. She felt as if his spirit had retreated somewhere far inside himself, to a place she couldn't follow. All she could do was hold tight to her husband's hand and wait.

Moments, hours, or a lifetime later—Nancy had no idea which—the police arrived. After examining the Toyota, the officer in charge barked, "Know of anyone who might have done this?"

Nancy gasped. "It—it's random, isn't it?" She clutched Damon's hand even tighter.

"Hardly." The officer pinned her with a lightning glance and pointed to the blood-red defacing. "This is racial. Someone obviously knows an African-American drives the car. Otherwise, the graffiti would be other obscenities as well."

"Graffiti!" Damon exploded.

"For want of a better word. Is there some place we can talk?"

"There certainly is." Increasing years had slowed Nicholas Fairchild's step but not his sharp mind or crisp voice. His wrath reflected on his face, the hospital director hurried toward them, along with the angry intern. "This is outrageous. We've had minor vandalism, but never anything like this."

Ten minutes later in the director's office, Nicholas repeated the statement and added, "What I don't understand is how Dr. Barton's car came to be targeted. He consults here, but is in private practice. If this is specifically aimed at Damon, how could the perpetrators know when he'd be here?"

The officer in charge laughed, but without mirth. "Perps— I mean, perpetrators—have ways of knowing a whole lot more than anyone gives them credit for. Dr. Barton, I asked you a question in the parking lot. Who might have it in for you? And why?"

Nancy's heart ached when the man she loved second only to God said in a dull voice, "My older brother turned state's evidence in a gang murder trial awhile back. Curtis and I look a lot alike. I suppose there may still be a few creeps out there holding a grudge."

"Naaa." The officer dismissed the stumbling explanation with the wave of a hand. "This is certainly not gang revenge. More likely the work of some white supremacist group. That kind of thing is increasing all the time, especially here in the Northwest. Bunches of fanatics recruit kids and teens. They start them out on hate stuff like this. They also brainwash them into thinking America will be a whole lot better off without Jews and anyone who is not Caucasian. Pretty soon they're carrying assault weapons and killing people who speak out against them."

Nancy's heart skipped a beat. She'd known about hate crimes, watched news reports, shuddered, and prayed for a day such hatred and sickness would be abolished forever. Yet even growing up in a less-than-desirable neighborhood hadn't pressed it in on her like the officer's rasping voice. Now she and Damon stood face-to-face with evil. Victims. Vulnerable. Sick at heart and powerless.

No! She would not allow predators to rob her of the belief most people were decent and all but a very small percentage could be reached if someone knew how. If she lost faith in her fellow human beings, it would surely affect her faith in God.

The officers started to leave, stern-faced and realistic. "Naturally, we'll try to find out who did this," the one in command promised. "Chances are we won't. The trees bordering the parking lot offer privacy. They also provide cover for someone bent on doing damage. The hospital can help out by beefing up security. Have the parking lots patrolled more, that kind of thing. Ironic, isn't it? All you want to do is help folks and this happens. Reminds me of what they did to a Man about 2,000 years ago who only wanted to help."

The officer's eyes bored into Damon who maintained a stony silence. "Be careful," he warned. He turned to Nancy. "You, too. I s'pose you have your own car." At her nod he continued. "If you ever at any time have the feeling you're being followed, head for the brightest lit street you can find and the nearest police station. *Don't go home.* And don't tell yourself you're being paranoid. Gut level feelings can save your life if you listen to what they're saying."

Her throat parched. "My life?"

"Yeah." The corners of his mouth turned down and he looked even grimmer. "You never know how many crazies there are out there unless you're a cop."

"Is she in danger because of me?" Damon burst out.

The officer shrugged. "Naaa. She may not be in danger at all." Compassion warmed his flinty eyes. "On the other hand, when white supremacists are involved, just being black is enough reason to be mighty careful."

No one spoke for a full moment after the police departed. Nancy still reeled with shock and ached for Damon, longing to cry out she would be fine and he wasn't to worry. Did

Nicholas Fairchild suspect her feelings? Perhaps. In any event, he cleared his throat and asked, "Do you need transportation?" A vision of the mutilated Toyota hung in the quiet room.

Nancy managed to say, "My car should be ready. The service manager knows me and will see it's delivered here when I call and explain. I—he can also send a tow truck." Was that thin voice hers, so in contrast to her usual rich tones?

"Let me," the director offered. He made the call and told Damon, "Whatever your insurance doesn't cover will be supplied by the hospital. I just can't say how sorry I am." His hand shot out in a warm grip.

Sight of the clasped hands, one dark, one light, brought a flood to Nancy's throat. It took all her training and self-control to keep from rushing out of the room. Instead, she took a deep breath, held it, then slowly released it. She must be strong for Damon's sake, when all she wanted to do was fling herself into her husband's arms and let his large body and soul protect her.

By the time the service manager personally delivered Nancy's red Honda, the hospital grapevine was in full swing. Shina and Patti raced to the Bartons like two full-strength tornadoes. Huffing and puffing as much with rage as from running, Patti's fierce hug nearly strangled Nancy.

"Of all the miserable, rotten things!" she erupted.

"Careful of your language," Shina reminded in a choked-up voice. "We're Christians, remember?" Her face crumpled. "Oh, Nancy." She threw her arms around the taller nurse. "How can anyone be so wicked?"

"I don't know." Her friends' warm support couldn't unfreeze the ice encasing Nancy's heart. It didn't melt even when they finally reached their apartment. But when Damon wordlessly turned to her and held out his arms, the great break-up began. She flew to him like a homing pigeon to its owner.

A long time later, he said, "It isn't just the damage to the car. It isn't even being called nigger. God knows I've had that enough times. It's the terrible hate mentality behind it."

Sheltered by his love, Nancy nodded. "I know. And it's the frightening knowledge the police feel someone, somewhere has been singling you or us out." In the security of his arms, she still shivered. "Damon, you don't think maybe this is just an isolated incident and the police could be wrong?"

"I hope so." The look in his eyes when he glanced down denied any real conviction. She saw the effort it took for him to say, "Woman, I'm starving. Do we eat out, call for takeout, or go out to the kitchen and see what we can find?"

His valiant attempt to lighten the conversation and lift their spirits called forth Nancy's admiration and determination to do the same. Even though eating out was the last thing she felt like doing, staying in the apartment surely meant more brooding. "I think we should climb into our Sunday best and go to a fantastic restaurant," she an-nounced. "If I wear the yellow two-piece dress you like, will you take me somewhere special, Dr. Barton? As special as you are?"

Damon laughed, not a masterpiece of its kind, but sufficient. "I'll call for reservations while you make yourself beau—even more beautiful."

"Thanks." Nancy kissed him soundly and reluctantly slid from his arms. "Surprise me," she told him on her way to their bedroom and adjoining bath. Damon rewarded her efforts with a genuine smile that took root in her troubled heart.

Before Nancy showered and changed into the promised yellow outfit, she knelt by the bed and talked with her Savior and Best Friend. She did not ask to be spared life's hardships. She never had. She simply prayed for courage and strength to face and conquer whatever life in a too often harsh world might bring.

"Please, God," she brokenly finished. "Help us meet each day the way Your Son who came to save us would do. We want to be Christlike, even when it seems impossible. In Jesus' name, amen."

Nancy raised her head, conscious of an unnatural stillness in the tasteful apartment living room. The feeling Damon was also on his knees, pouring out his soul before the throne of God, kept her from going to him. At bedtime, they would kneel hand-in-hand, as they had done every night since their wedding. For now, each must fly solo on wings of prayer to meet their Heavenly Father.

Humming a favorite chorus, Nancy showered and changed. The cleansing water and knowledge she dressed for her husband helped the shattering events of the day recede until they seemed like a bad dream. So did Damon's determined cheerfulness. Yet when they climbed into Nancy's car, neither glanced at the empty stall in the parking garage where a late model white Toyota usually sat companionably close to a red Honda.

two

When Nancy closed the apartment door, she also slammed the door of her mind on problems. *I'll do everything I can to salvage at least some remnants of what began as a perfect day,* she silently promised herself.

Damon held the car door for her and she laughed up at him. "So where are we going?" She could see twin reflections of her yellow self in his dark eyes.

Damon grinned. "You're always so color coordinated I considered taking you to McDonald's for hamburgers." She groaned and he added, "Don't worry. I reconsidered."

"I hope so. This is a party, not a grab-and-gulp meal." She patted his cheek and slid into the car. "On second thought, don't tell me."

"Okay." Damon dropped a kiss on her cheek, closed her door, and strode around the car. Inside and seat-belted, he backed from the garage and expertly merged with the evening traffic. "I hope you can hold out for a short drive."

"I'm hungry, but I can't think of anything I'd like better than a drive," Nancy told him. Deadly weariness descended on her. She slumped against her seat belt, and leaned back against the headrest. "Pediatrics was a circus this afternoon. Too many patients on their way to recovery. Not that I mind." She laughed and felt better. "Isn't it funny? I seldom care for a child who doesn't grow more demanding when they're starting to get well."

Damon took advantage of a break in traffic to briefly squeeze her hand. "Not just kids!" He chuckled and a lecturing note came into his voice. "Nurse Nancy, there are two kinds of men. One kind wants everyone to wait on them when they're sick. The others just want to be left alone."

"Which kind are you, professor?" she teased.

"Thank God I'm seldom ill," he fervently told her. "When I am, I get crankier than a bear with a sore paw."

"In that event, remind me to leave you strictly alone should you catch any kind of bug," Nancy retorted. His hearty laugh chased away some of her fatigue and she glanced out the window. "I know where we're going. Anthony's Homeport at the Des Moines Marina, right?"

"Right." Damon concentrated on his driving while Nancy enjoyed the ending day. The setting sun turned fleecy clouds and the water of Puget Sound rose and old gold. Tree-covered Vashon Island lazily stretched out a short distance away. Nancy, tuned to appreciation of God's perfect creation, felt peace steal into her heart, just as it had when she prayed earlier. With all the beauty in the world, why must there be the ugliness of sin? She clamped down hard on the thought and pushed it out of her mind. She and Damon might not be able to change the world. They could change their own world. One way was to refuse to allow others to dictate their lives.

"Barton, reservation for two," Damon told the hostess after they climbed to the upper level of Anthony's, one of their favorite seafood restaurants. "I hope you have a window table for us."

"We do, sir. It will be just a few moments."

"Thank you." Damon led Nancy to a padded seat in front of flickering flames in a large fireplace. He turned her toward a nearby mirror and threw an arm over her shoulders. "That's an awfully good-looking couple, don't you think?"

Nancy cocked her head to one side and observed the tall young nurse in yellow and the taller young doctor whose charcoal suit fit so well.

"Of course."

A slight movement drew her attention to the reflection next to theirs. Was it a distortion in the glass that made the stranger appear to be wearing a disgusted expression when his gaze met hers? Or the angle at which he held his closely-cropped head? That couldn't be active dislike in the man's face, could it? If so, why? She had never seen him before.

The next instant the stranger moved. His face went bland and his gaze shifted from Nancy's. She automatically glanced at Damon' reflection. His untroubled dark eyes showed he had seen nothing, if indeed there had been anything to see.

"Right this way," the hostess said.

Shaken by unexplainable dread hanging over her like a pall, Nancy numbly followed to a window table that overlooked the marina and the water. Her brain whirled. Even if the unfriendly man felt disgusted, it probably had nothing to do with the Bartons. Some people had a fetish about conceit. Perhaps the stranger had missed the teasing undertones in the laughing conversation. Goodness, today's incident wasn't going to make her so suspicious she saw dislike in every casual glance, was it?

Nancy bit her lip and stared at the sparkling white table-cloth, the shining silver, the small vase of fresh spring flowers. Why must the police officer's warning, *Don't tell yourself you're being paranoid* come to mind here at this lovely restaurant? Nevertheless, she furtively glanced back toward the lobby and felt secretly relieved. The man who had stared so was being ushered to the opposite end of the dining room from where she and Damon sat.

"Something to drink?" the hostess inquired.

"Just water, please." Damon smiled at her.

"Very good." She removed the wine glasses from the table. "Your waiter will be right with you."

He turned toward the large window. "Impressive, isn't it?"

"Yes. I never tire of coming here," Nancy said in a low voice.

It was more than impressive. Below them, a fleet of vari-sized, anchored boats rose and fell with the gentle waves from those heading in before nightfall. A large sailboat gently drifted toward them. In the distance, gleaming white ferry boats plowed the waters of the Sound, filled with commuters on their way home at the end of another day's work in Seattle. A small yacht bound for Tacoma or points south grew smaller and became a mere speck on the horizon.

Nancy sighed and quickly covered it with a laugh. Now was not the time for melancholy. With a quick prayer for strength, she feigned enthusiasm over the menu and ordering. She did not have to pretend when it came to eating. Her system hungrily accepted the crisp salad, excellent sourdough bread, and perfectly grilled salmon. She appreciated equally her small new potatoes and a medley of fresh, steamed vegetables.

"Have I told you I admire your appetite, along with a few dozen other things?" Damon teased when they spooned up the last bites of their burnt cream.

Nancy raised an eyebrow and unobtrusively patted her well-filled stomach. "Will you still feel that way when I weigh a ton? A few more dinners like this and I just may."

A poignant light brightened her husband's eyes. He reached across the small table, took her hand, and said in a low and husky voice, "Nancy Galbraith Barton, I married you for better or for worse. Nothing will ever change my love."

"Nor mine," she whispered. For the second time that day, she longed to grasp the moment with fingers of steel and never let go. All she could do was file it in the memory cabinet of her heart. She overcame some of the sadness of its departure by knowing she would bring the moment out and savor it again and again, long after the March day joined its ancestors and vanished forever.

Hours later, Nancy awakened from deep, surprisingly untroubled sleep. What had disturbed her? She reached to the other side of the bed. "Damon?"

"I'm here." He sounded far more alert than she.

"Have you been asleep?"

"No."

"Shall I warm you some milk? Or make hot chocolate?"

"No." He shifted restlessly beside her. "This trouble isn't going to go away just because we ignore it." He sounded depressed.

"I know." Nancy switched on her bedside lamp. Its soft glow showed Damon propped up on his pillow, arms crossed behind his head. "We aren't sure it's aimed directly at you or that it's racial," she said, wanting to believe her statement but not succeeding. "Maybe someone you've had to reprimand for sloppy work wanted to get even. It could be a patient or relative who didn't like the care you gave."

"Don't, Nancy. Please. I appreciate what you're trying to do, but playing ostrich and sticking our heads in the sand won't solve the problem. Especially if this is just the beginning." His eyes looked dull with misgiving.

Fear gripped her throat. She sat bolt upright. "The beginning?"

Damon reached for her and cradled her in his arms. "We have to be realistic. Even though the police don't consider it gang-related, someone wanted to hurt me, maybe send a message. He or they wanted it badly enough to either watch for me or follow me." His forehead wrinkled. "By me, I mean me as Dr. Barton or as an African-American. Either way, there's an unseen enemy out there who is obviously stalking me. It would be a lot easier if I knew."

Nancy felt tremors go from the soles of her feet to the top of her head. "Do you really think there will be other incidents?" Her uneven voice pleaded with him to say no, to reassure her that the offender or offenders would be satisfied with disfiguring the car. Yet the neighborhood in which she had grown up denied her any such comfort. Vicious attacks generated other, usually worse attacks, especially if more than one person became involved.

"We may be called on to be stronger than we've ever been in our lives," Damon warned. "The one thing others can't control is the choices we make on how to respond." He laughed. "Although I am not ready to pray for the persons responsible."

"Neither am I. Maybe tomorrow." She snuggled closer. "Darling, as long as we have God and each other, we'll make it. No matter what."

"I know, and I thank Him," Damon whispered. Warmed by their faith and love, at last they slept.

With the morning came hope. At lunch Nancy confided to Shina and Patti, "That March wind would blow the cobwebs out of anyone's brain. You two look like spring itself."

"Don't we?" Patti touched her lavender pants outfit, then motioned toward Shina's mint green. "I like your pale pink, Nancy. It looks like the underside of an apple blossom. How come no yellow? You aren't tired of looking like a sunbeam, are you? I'm sure that's what attracted Dr. Barton."

Shina gasped at Patti's kidding but Nancy only laughed. "Damon likes me in pink and peach, too. Actually, Damon loves me no matter what I wear."

"But he likes you best in yellow," the blonde nurse insisted.

"Patti Thompson, where are your manners?" Shina burst out.

Nancy forestalled an answer by pointing past the crisp white curtains framing the windows of the green-painted Shepherd of Love staff dining room. Whipping branches and dancing daffodils showed against sapphire sky and fresh-born spring grass. "I have to confess, I love it."

"Me, too," Patti said ungrammatically. "Except I'd rather be out walking in the wind instead of sitting inside and looking at it." She raised her hands above her head in a stretch. "Remember Christina Rossetti's poem?

Who has seen the wind?
Neither you nor I.

But when the trees bow down their heads
   The wind is passing by.

"I'd love to be out in it. Hey, speaking of out, did you find out anything more about the creep who trashed your car?" Patti asked with more bluntness than tact. "I hope they nab him and throw the book at him, and not a poetry book!"

"Maybe it's a her," Shina volunteered. Nancy suspected the tiny nurse had seen her involuntary twinge and was trying to lighten things up. Shina confirmed it when she sent Patti a warning glance and added, "Since you're such a student, Patti, tell me. Would a lady—excuse me, a female—creep, be a creepette? A creepess, maybe?"

Nancy laughed in spite of herself. "How you can look so solemn and come out with something like that is beyond me."

"It's part of my fatal charm." Shina smirked, looked at the ceiling and clutched in the general region of her heart.

"Hey, that's my line," Patti objected.

"Now that your long-suffering roomie Lindsey is Mrs. Chaplain Terence O'Shea, someone has to keep you in line," Shina loftily announced.

Her blonde friend crossed her eyes and retorted, "The moral of the story is to be careful how you pray."

"What!" Nancy and Shina both stared.

Patti grinned and frankly told them, "Well, it's true. I prayed for patience and God sent Shina, didn't He?"

Shina had the last word. "Too bad He didn't also send patience." The next instant she sobered. Patti, obviously intent on coming up with a scathing reply, didn't seem to notice. Nancy did. It was the same look she had seen earlier. Laugh and joke as she might, Shina Ito carried a hidden burden.

Shina glanced at Nancy and almost imperceptibly shook her head. The signal stilled Nancy's sympathetic question. So did the plea for understanding in the midnight-black eyes. Nancy nodded. Relief replaced the apprehension and showed when Shina felt ready to speak, she knew Nancy would be there for her.

The Pediatrics nurse left the other two good-naturedly sparring for the benefit of an unmarried resident and two single interns who came to the table.

"A little bit of nonsense can make a whole lot of difference," she murmured.

The afternoon proved too busy for either nonsense or worry. Nurse Nancy, as her young charges called her, found the capricious March wind no more unruly than some of her patients. "I'm glad we're discharging three of them as soon as Dr. Barton comes. I'll bet you are, too." She raised a cup of coffee during a quick break and smiled at the licensed practical nurse on whom she greatly depended. "You have most of the hands-on care for them, Susan."

The forty-something LPN chuckled. "Right." Her brown eyes twinkled. "That's why I never had any desire to become an RN. Too much administrative stuff and not enough nursing, for me. Although I notice you still find time to do patient care." Her motherly smile warmed Nancy thoroughly.

"I love it. Kids, too. Damon and I plan to have a houseful someday." She felt color mount to her smooth cheeks.

"Get a house first," Susan Devers advised. "You can raise kids in apartments but it's nice to have a place for them to run. Any luck so far?"

Nancy shook her head. "The old story. Wants versus money." She caught the LPN's sidewise glance. "I suppose everyone thinks that we have a bundle because Damon's in private practice with Dr. Cranston and I work. But we don't."

Susan raised sandy eyebrows that matched her hair. "It really isn't anyone's business, is it? Besides, word gets around. Shepherd of Love Hospital isn't the only one who gives necessary medical care, even costly special treatments to those who can't afford to pay." She glanced down, then back at Nancy. "Including those from the inner city who come to the downtown Sanctuary and Care Center where you and Dr. Barton volunteer."

"You do keep informed, don't you?" Nancy accused.

Susan remained serious. "Parents whose kids get help they couldn't pay for in a thousand years are mighty grateful. They talk." She paused. "You may never know how many lives will be changed through a kind deed. One thing more: you can't out-give God. Even when we're called to make what we see as sacrifices, they're nothing compared with what He does for us." She glanced at her nurse's watch. "Time to go back to work."

Nancy blinked hard. "Thanks, pal."

"For what?" Susan's eyes rounded in astonishment.

An outcry from the ward effectively ended the conversation, but Nancy treasured the brief break. She tackled a stack of charts with fresh vigor and completed them a few minutes before Damon was due to arrive. She also took time to slip into the staff rest room, straighten her uniform, and smooth her hair. "It's absurd for an old married woman like you to allow her heart to beat as furiously as a teenager waiting for her first date," she scolded the mischievous face peering back at her from the mirror over the sink. "Utterly absurd."

It didn't help a bit. Just the sight of a certain Dr. Barton striding down the corridor toward her always made Nancy weak in the knees.

"Thank You, God, for Damon," she whispered, and went back to the nurses' station, positioned like a hub in the center of the Pediatrics department. Wards and a few separate rooms encircled it. Shepherd of Love and the Pediatrics staff believed children recuperated faster when they could be with other children. The private and semi-private rooms were reserved for serious and contagious cases, or overflow from the wards during extremely busy time periods.

Nancy loved being in the center of things. From the command post, she could keep an eye on her staff and patients.

The sound of laughter, an occasional cry, the plaintive, "Nurth Nanthy" of lisping children sang in her ears and heart.

"I'm like a queen surveying her domain," she often happily told her husband. A smile of anticipation tilted her lips. If it didn't take too long for Damon to check out those patients under his care, perhaps he'd take her on their delayed house-hunting expedition.

"Wonder what kind of day he had," she mused. "I hope it was as nice as mine." Yet as the hands of the wall clock behind her desk relentlessly crept toward the time set for his arrival, Nancy discovered she stood with hands clenched. Her first glimpse of Damon would tell whether he had been able to lose himself in work and at least temporarily put yesterday's miserable business behind him, as she had done.

She glanced from clock to her watch. Had Juliet felt like this, waiting for Romeo? Nancy quietly laughed at the comparison. She and Damon were not star-crossed literary teenage lovers, but living, breathing persons dedicated to helping others, ministering in Christ's stead and for His glory—not their own.

The second hands of watch and clock went on and on. The minute hands followed, steadily ticking off the time. Five, ten, fifteen minutes.

Damon did not come.

The swing shift arrived, fresh from the prayer service Shepherd of Love Hospital personnel attended before going on duty.

Damon still did not come.

"Your boyfriend stand you up?" a nursing assistant asked, eyes twinkling.

"Shoo." Susan Devers motioned her away. "You have plenty to do without hassling the supervisors." The girl laughed and moved off. Susan pretended extreme busyness, obviously reluctant to leave.

A half hour into evening shift, Nancy told Susan to go home. "There's nothing you can do here," she said in a calm voice that didn't fool either of them. "Obviously, he's been delayed. I'll call Dr. Cranston's office."

Susan lingered. The phone rang several times, but no one answered. Where was everyone? Nancy wondered. Why didn't the office answering machine switch on?

Nancy broke the connection and redialed with shaking fingers. Susan took an involuntary step toward the rigid figure.

An eternity later, Damon answered. He sounded so ragged and faraway, Nancy barely recognized his voice.

three

The morning after the incident in the hospital lot, Dr. Damon Barton took no chances. He parked in front of the hospital staff entrance, kissed Nancy good-bye, and waited until she stepped inside Shepherd of Love. She would be safe there.

A chill went through him. Would she? Nicholas Fairchild and the board of directors believed they had weeded out all who had been involved in the earlier attempted hospital takeover. Suppose they were wrong. How could he protect the woman he loved more than life? What if his best were not good enough?

All the way from Shepherd of Love to the office suite he shared with Dr. Cranston, Damon mulled over the previous day's trouble. If only he could believe there would be no more such happenings. His jaw set in a hard line as he parked, turned off the ignition, and bowed his head.

"God, I'll do everything I can," he promised. "Please, surround Nancy with Your protection when we're apart. She's been hurt enough." Visions of the terrible fire in which Nancy lost her mother and sister danced in his mind. It took great effort to push them aside. "I'm going to need a whole lot of help in order to forgive," he confessed.

Damon stopped short. He couldn't continue without feeling like a hypocrite. Forgiving his unknown enemies was one thing. Learning to forgive anyone who harmed or terrified Nancy was a different story, one for which he had no ending. On their wedding day, Nancy's trusting dark eyes had called forth the chivalry practiced in the days of knights and their ladies. Damon grunted. Even then he had known Nancy was no fragile reed to be easily broken. Yet he had silently pledged

28

himself to defend her.

Now he clenched a strong hand and pounded on the seat beside him.

"At least in the olden days, challengers recognized their enemies. They could ride forth and do battle with them. How can a man fight creeping, insidious evil, the powers and principalities Paul warns against in Ephesians six?"

The troubled man stepped from the Honda and slowly walked to the front door of the office building. With the ease of long practice, he parked his problems outside the door as expertly as he had parked the red Honda. Once he stepped inside, he was all doctor.

Back-to-back morning appointments kept him too busy to brood. When Dr. Cranston poked his head in the office door and said, "I'm finally free. Can you break for a late lunch?" Damon glanced at the clock.

"Two o'clock? Where did the time go? Don't Seattle parents patronize any child specialists except us?"

The older doctor, who had made a name for himself through equal parts determination to help children and plain old-fashioned hard work, grinned and stretched. Yet after they reached their favorite nearby deli, Dr. Cranston glanced at Damon over hearty salads and steaming bowls of homemade soup.

"All right. What is it?"

Damon grimaced. "Trying to hide anything from you is futile." The joy of his morning's work fled. "Yesterday at Shepherd of Love someone trashed my car." He viciously attacked a chunk of lettuce, but didn't pick it up. "All four tires slashed. Writing on the car." He put down his fork, appetite gone.

"What kind of writing?" Dr. Cranston barked.

"*NIGGER.* Spray-painted in blood red, a half-dozen times," Damon spit out.

"I'm not surprised."

Blood rushed to Damon's head. He stared at Dr. Cranston, his mouth so dry it felt like he'd swallowed the Sahara Desert.

"Excuse me?" he croaked.

Dr. Cranston's eyes flashed fire. "I said I'm not surprised." He fumbled in the vest pocket of his well-cut suit, brought out a creased paper, and shoved it across the table.

Damon gritted his teeth and unfolded the single sheet. Warned by his friend and mentor's ominous silence, he fully expected a message made of letters cut from newspapers or magazines, such as those shown in TV crime shows. Instead, ugly words sprawled across the page, the handwriting bold and black.

GET RID OF YOUR NIGGER ASSOCIATE OR TAKE THE CONSEQUENCES AND BE RESPONSIBLE FOR WHAT FOLLOWS.

The message barely registered in Damon's stunned brain. The handwriting did. Only one man of his acquaintance wrote in such a slanting scrawl: *the doctor calmly sitting across the table from him.*

For a moment, Damon thought he'd be sick. "I don't understand."

"Phone call last night at home," Dr. Cranston said briefly. "I jotted it down so I wouldn't forget a single word."

Shame for harboring doubts about one of the best friends Damon had ever known warred with alarm for control of Damon's brain.

"You say you got this last night at home? Then the car wasn't just an isolated incident aimed at just any African-American. I'm definitely the target. Why didn't you tell me?"

Dr. Cranston met Damon's steady gaze without wavering. "I'm not easily scared by anonymous threats. Besides, I had no idea something else had happened. I notified the police. There was no way they could trace the call." He looked puzzled. "What I don't understand is how whoever is responsible obtained my home number. It's unlisted and always has been."

"They have ways." Damon took a deep breath and slowly released it. "Maybe you should."

"Should what?"

Damon's mouth tasted like sour ashes. "Get rid of me."

"In a pig's eye!" Dr. Cranston leaned forward and shook a long finger in Damon's face. "Think I'm going to let a threat from someone who doesn't have the guts to use his name make me oust the finest specialist I know?" Incredulity gave way to fury. "Even if you were the greenest intern who ever held a scalpel, I wouldn't let you go. I refuse to be intimidated, do you hear?"

Damon's taut nerves relaxed into a whoop of laughter. "Me and most of downtown Seattle!" He inclined his head toward the other occupants of the deli. Most sat staring with open mouths. The one exception was a man with close-cropped hair who stolidly went on eating as if it were his last meal.

"Anything wrong, doctors?" the owner called from behind the counter.

"Not a thing," Dr. Cranston bellowed back. "I'm just reminding Dr. Barton how important it is to not allow others to run our lives. Or ruin them."

"Good for you, Doc." The burly proprietor waved a gleaming spatula, then turned to the grill and flipped two burgers. "That's just what I always say. If folks'd mind their own business instead of everyone else's, this old world would be a better place."

Damon felt his skin scorch from the attention they were getting from the deli's other patrons.

"Uh, are you about finished? I have to go back to the office before leaving for Shepherd of Love. Three of my patients are ready to be discharged, but I want to check them once more before signing them out."

Dr. Cranston raised one eyebrow at Damon's uneaten meal and thrust his own half-filled plate of salad away. "I've had enough." Despite Damon's objections, he tossed down money for both lunches and the tip. "You drove. I'll pay."

Damon never knew what caused him to turn and look back when they reached the door. His casual glance met and locked with that of the stolid man, who had stood and was pulling on a Seattle Mariners' cap. Heavy-lidded eyes bore into Damon like augers into soft wood before changing to deliberate blankness. The man turned his back and stepped toward the cash register.

Dr. Barton started to speak of it to Dr. Cranston, then bit his tongue. Why waste time discussing a stranger neither of them would ever see again? The man wasn't a regular at the deli; at least Damon didn't remember having seen him there. He shrugged and followed his friend to Nancy's red Honda.

"We can't just ignore it," Damon remarked once they merged into the steady flow of traffic. "If my being your partner is going to endanger you in any way, I'm out of here." A lightning glance at Dr. Cranston caught his friend's smirk.

"Forget it. You have a contract, remember?"

"Better to break a contract than have something happen to you," Damon moodily told him. He shot another quick look at his companion.

Not a trace of humor remained in the kindly face. Or in Robert Cranston's voice when he said, "Look, Damon. I've lived too long to run from a good fight. It appears that's exactly what we're facing. Don't argue," he ordered when Damon started to protest. "This isn't just your fight. Hatred, prejudice, and bigotry are the concern of every decent human being. We're going to get to the bottom of this, no matter what it takes or how long. Agreed?"

Damon inhaled sharply, then said, "You are magnificent."

"So I've been telling people for years. Nice someone is finally listening. Now, about that latest referral from the Sanctuary and Care Center. . ." Dr. Cranston went on to discuss the new case, keeping the subject firmly changed during the short drive back to their office suite. "One of the best things Shepherd of Love ever did was start the Center downtown," he finished. "Union Gospel Mission, the Salvation Army, and other fine organizations need all the help they can get." His eyebrows met in a frown. "Funny, isn't it? Cities, not just Seattle, find money to build stadiums and ball parks. On the other hand, there never seems to be funds available to construct shelters so people won't go hungry, or freeze to death during hard winters."

"I know how you feel," Damon admitted. "I like a good ball game as much as anyone else. I want Seattle to keep its teams. Yet sometimes I wonder. Will we be held more accountable for what we fail to do—in this case, provide for the homeless and down-and-out—than for wrongdoing?" He glanced at his watch. "We don't have time to solve the world's problems today. My patients and Nancy are waiting for me."

A small smile lingered on his sensitively curved lips. In a moment of rare confidence he added, "It's pretty wonderful seeing a woman's face light up at the end of the day when her man comes home, isn't it?" He stopped, half-ashamed of showing sentiment but thrilling to the thought of Nancy walking toward him from the nurses' station that oversaw Pediatrics.

"It is." Dr. Cranston sounded gruff, but Damon saw the understanding gleam in his keen eyes.

Laughing like schoolboys, they reached their office suite. Laughter and Damon's uplifted mood vanished like Puget Sound fog chased by a brisk north wind. Their capable office nurse Janet McIntyre huddled against the wall next to the open door, face white and twisted.

"What's wrong?" Dr. Cranston demanded. "Are you sick?"

She licked her lips and shook her head. "No. It's—I swear, I was only gone for a little while, and. . ."

"Gone? Gone where?"

The pleasant-faced, thirtyish nurse straightened, obviously attempting to get control of herself.

"After you left, I told Paige I'd watch the office while she went to lunch."

Nothing out of the ordinary there, Damon knew. The nurse and receptionist always staggered their lunch breaks so someone would be in the office. Dr. Cranston disliked the impersonal, seemingly uncaring feeling an answering machine gave parents whose children needed help.

"A few minutes after Paige left, the call came." Janet wiped her eyes but one drop escaped. "An excited voice, I couldn't tell if it were male or female, said there had been an accident just a block from here. It mumbled something about a doctor being hurt and that help was needed immediately." Her eyes grew enormous. "I dialed 911, gave the information and ran out." A dull, red flush spread from the collar of her neat blue uniform to her pulled-back dark hair. She looked miserable. "I was so afraid it might be one of you, I forgot to lock the office door. I'm so sorry."

"Never mind that," Damon said. "What about the accident?"

"There was no accident!" Janet's shoulders sagged and worry filled her face. "I had to wait until 911 responded so I could tell them it must be a hoax, but it couldn't have been more than twenty minutes. When I returned, I found. . ." She wordlessly gestured inside. "The phone's been ringing, but I didn't know if I should touch anything, what with—"

Damon cut short her halting explanation by bolting into the reception area of the office suite, closely followed by Dr. Cranston. Shock throttled him. He barely heard the other doctor's bellow of rage. How could anyone do this amount of damage in twenty minutes?

It looked like a film scene of a World War II Nazi search. Paige's desk had been swept clean. The contents sprawled on the carpet. File drawers lay upended beside them.

"I'll stake my life that's the same blood-red spray paint

that's on my Toyota," Damon muttered. The word *NIGGER* dominated the defilement of the warm cream walls and rare paintings, but the worst obscenities Damon had ever heard accompanied them, marring the doors to various adjoining offices with their filth.

"You saw no one at any time?" Dr. Cranston asked Janet.

"No." Tears welled into her eyes. "It's so vile and it's my fault."

Damon spun on his heel. "This is not your fault in any way, Janet. Whoever did this obviously set the whole thing up. Someone who knows our office routine and personnel saw me leave with Dr. Cranston. He or she—although it's hard to believe a woman is responsible—also saw Paige go."

Fresh horror sprang to Janet's eyes. She took a step backward. "We're being watched?"

"Yes." He glanced at the other doctor. "You might as well know the whole thing." He quickly filled the nurse in on the vandalism to his car at Shepherd of Love. Dr. Cranston showed her the warning note.

To Damon's utter amazement, instead of increasing fear, the incidents aroused Janet's courage like a shot of epinephrine stimulates the heart. Her shoulders shot back. Her head snapped as smartly as a soldier to attention. "Well! Then we'll just have to find out who's responsible, won't we?"

The phone rang sharply from its position on the floor. Damon reached for it, but Dr. Cranston's iron grip seized his wrist. "Use a handkerchief, in case there are prints," he ordered.

By the time Damon pulled a spotless handkerchief from his pocket and gingerly picked up the receiver, all he got was a dial tone. He cradled it. It rang again. This time he was prepared. "Cranston and Barton." His heart galloped. His skin crawled with sweat. He clutched the phone, half-expecting a jeering laugh or cruel taunt concerning the invasion. Dr. Cranston and Janet stood motionless as the statues of early pioneers that adorned various Seattle parks.

"Damon?"

Relief flooded through him. "Thank God it's you, Nancy." To offset his fervent greeting, he hastily added, "Something's come up, don't know when I can get there. Don't leave the hospital until I come." He checked the time on a wall clock that had somehow escaped the destruction. "Patti or Shina should be going to supper soon. Go with them, then to one of their rooms. Okay?"

"Okay."

Damon could tell by Nancy's quick intake of breath he hadn't fooled her into thinking his delay came from a trivial thing. He silently blessed her for not being a person who demanded explanations under every circumstance. He moved his mouth closer to the phone, taking care not to touch it with his lips. "I love you, darling." Her soft affirmation alerted him to the fact others must be close by and she wasn't free to talk.

"Call the police," Robert Cranston said when he broke the connection.

Damon obeyed, briefly stating there had been a break-in and vandalism. The dispatcher on the other end of the line promised to send officers at once.

A slight sound whipped the three occupants of the room toward the doorway. Paige Jones stood open-mouthed. Her purse slipped from nerveless fingers and joined the clutter on the floor.

"What on earth!" Her blue eyes stared at the reception area as if hypnotized.

Janet McIntyre said in a nearly normal voice, "I'll fill Paige in. You two should check the rest of the place." Dread returned to her face.

By mutual consent they examined one office at a time, as if seeking support should they find more chaos. To Damon's infinite relief, only the main office had been attacked.

"The creep or creeps probably gauged the time element," Dr. Cranston commented. "But in broad daylight? It's completely foolhardy."

"Or an arrogant declaration someone feels above the law and laughs at it," Damon somberly said. He repeated the same thing to the police when they came and saw by their quick exchange of glances they privately agreed.

"This is bad enough but it could have been worse," they warned. "Dr. Barton, you say this isn't the first problem?"

Damon wondered if they would ever finish questioning him. Long after the officers sent a staunchly-supportive Janet and a terrified, but clearly excited Paige home, they continued to go over the entire afternoon.

"Is there anything, no matter how slight, you haven't told us?" the officer in charge finally asked.

Bone-weary, knowing Nancy would be almost out of her mind wondering why he didn't come, Damon shook his head. Still, something stirred. "Oh. It's probably nothing, but a guy at the deli looked at me kind of funny when I started out, then turned back. I feel kind of stupid even mentioning it, but you said—"

"Description?" The officer waited, pen poised above a notebook in which he'd already scrawled pages of illegible-looking notes.

Damon closed his eyes and conjured up a clear image of the stranger's face. "Stolid. Close-cropped hair. Only person who didn't look up when our conversation got kind of loud. Seattle Mariners' cap. Heavy-lidded eyes that bore into me, then looked as if he had pulled down a shade."

"He was there when you arrived and didn't leave until after you did?"

"Correct." Damon felt his heart skip a beat. "If he's involved, it means there must be at least two persons in on this. Anger-Eyes couldn't have made the call or trashed this place. Maybe he's just a guy who tries to prove something by staring people down."

The officer smiled curiously. "It may be nothing, but we'll want you to work with a staff artist and see what you can come up with. Okay?"

"Of course." Damon stood and stretched his kinked muscles. "May I make it later this evening? My wife got off duty at Shepherd of Love Hospital hours ago. I told her to wait there until I came." His voice hardened. "No way do I want her getting a ride and going home to an empty apartment. I'll bring her with me."

"You're a very wise man," the officer said. "Observant, too." He shook hands with Damon. "Pick up your wife. Get yourselves some dinner and come to the station when you can." He turned to Dr. Cranston. "Anything else?"

"No. I didn't notice Anger-Eyes, as Damon called him." Cranston sighed. "Wish I had. On the other hand, there's no reason I would. From what Damon says, the guy didn't wink an eyelash until he thought we were out the door."

"Right." The officer snapped his notebook shut. "Interesting, isn't it?"

four

Nancy cradled the phone and stared at Susan Devers.

"Well?" Susan demanded.

"Damon said something has come up. He isn't sure how long he will be."

The LPN relaxed. "No problem. I'll be happy to take you home."

Nancy shook her head. "Damon asked me to wait for him here. He didn't say why." Fear oozed through her. "Something more must have happened. I've gone home by myself dozens of times when Damon was delayed. Why would he practically order me to find Shina or Patti and stay at the hospital?"

"Beats me." Susan shrugged and tossed her head but it didn't fool Nancy, not even when she added, "Maybe Dr. Barton simply prefers that you don't ride with anyone else."

The unspoken words *after what happened* hung in the air between them.

Nancy squared her shoulders.

"Thanks for trying, but we both know it has to be more than that."

"I'll be happy to stick around," Susan offered.

"Thanks, but it isn't necessary. However, if you think I need a bodyguard, you may walk me to the dining room and turn me over to the wardens, I mean, Patti and Shina," Nancy teased, a triumph of will over her whirling emotions.

"Don't think I won't," the capable nurse said grimly. She quickly covered it up with a laugh. "Forward, march, prisoner."

Pediatrics, part of the Family Center, occupied an entire side of the second floor of the hospital, along with Parenting

Education, Labor and Delivery, Recovery, and Children's Therapy. Nancy and Shina often met on their way off duty at the end of their shifts. Today the tiny nurse would already be gone. Why should Nancy be secretly relieved Susan had insisted on shepherding her down the curving stairway? What was she, a kindergartner to be led by her mother to where she was supposed to go? She grinned at the thought and felt a little better.

They crossed the Central Waiting Area, furnished with comfortable seating and an abundance of Christian reading material, then walked down the hall to the staff dining room. Susan stubbornly refused to leave until Nancy gave her an affectionate little push and pointed.

"Shina and Patti are both inside. I'll be fine."

She rested her dark hand on Susan's freckled arm. "Thanks."

"Any time. If I didn't have a husband who will be coming home for dinner soon, I'd join you." She sniffed. "Shepherd of Love does itself proud when it comes to eats. See you tomorrow." She started away, then swung back. "Take care of yourself, Nancy. You and Dr. Barton are too special to lose." Susan hurried off, giving Nancy no chance to reply.

Taking a deep breath, Nancy pasted on a smile and walked into the dining room. Graceful steps took her to a linen-covered table with its bouquet of fresh flowers and a bevy of laughing medical personnel hungrily attacking dinner.

"As I live and breathe, if it isn't Nancy Galbraith Barton in person!" Patti Thompson's blue eyes rounded in pretend awe. "To what do we owe this unexpected pleasure?"

"Damon will be late so it gives me a chance to honor you with my presence," Nancy told her. She ducked her head and dropped her purse to an empty chair. "Mmm. Smells good. I'll be back." She headed for the tastefully arranged buffet Shepherd of Love offered rather than cafeteria-style meals.

Please, God, help me be able to eat and not let on any-thing's wrong, Nancy prayed while forcing herself to select food. Explaining to Shina and Patti would be hard enough. She couldn't and wouldn't discuss her fears at the table.

Nancy need not have worried. The usual circle of unmarried doctors who flocked around pert blond Patti and sparkling Shina teased them unmercifully. Their banter allowed Nancy to eat in peace. After poking the first few bites down, she was able to eat the rest of her dinner.

When the male contingent reluctantly tore themselves away from the table, Nancy casually asked, "Are you two busy? Damon didn't know when he could pick me up."

"And you'd rather not go home alone," Patti said thoughtlessly. The next moment she looked contrite. Her eyes turned to shimmering lakes. "I shouldn't have said that. You probably are trying to forget yesterday."

Nancy noticed Shina's look of dismay and quickly answered, "Something like that. So are you free?"

"I have a date, but I can break it," Patti offered. Her eyes darkened. "I really wouldn't mind."

"Charles would," Shina told her. "I am fully capable of entertaining Nancy without your help."

"Who is Charles?" Nancy inquired, glad for the change of subject. "The ambulance driver? No, his name's Mike, isn't it?"

"That was last month's love interest," Shina teased.

Patti turned pink, but she laughed. "I barely know Charles. He came into Outpatient with a friend. Charles is a pilot. Maybe he will teach me to fly."

Shina giggled. "You mean you aren't angelic enough to make it on your own?" She rolled her eyes. "After all you've been telling me."

"You are totally impossible." Patti pushed her chair back and got up. "I really will break my date if you need us, Nancy."

"Not us as in both. Us as in one of us. Me," Shina put in. "Run along and get ready or you'll be late."

"Yes, mother," Patti chuckled and bounced off.

"It's nice to see her like this again," Nancy also rose. "Let's go to your room, okay? I'm a little surprised you haven't moved in with Patti now that Lindsey's married. She must get lonely in the double."

"We discussed it," Shina said on the way to the staff residence hall, built in the form of a T. The two-story building was attached to the hospital by a covered passageway that led to the middle of the lower floor in the center of the T's crossbar. It opened on a lovely living room, with a library on one side, and a recreation room and small laundry on the other. The long part of the T had small apartments. Female employees who chose to live on the grounds occupied the ground floor; males lived upstairs.

"You decided against it?" Nancy asked.

"Actually, Patti made the decision." Shina led the way to her charming yellow single, close to the rose suite where Nancy lived before she got married.

"Really?" Nancy dropped to the couch in the immaculate living room.

"Yes, and it's probably for the best." Shina's whole face lit up when she smiled. "Patti said she didn't want to hurt my feelings, but she knew if we lived together, she'd lean on me the way she did with Lindsey when they shared the apartment. She would, too," the small nurse said. "Patti has always been too easily swayed by others. She's beginning to recognize and work on it, though. She told me she needed to be independent because one of these times Mr. Right is going to show up and she needs to be more than a clinging vine."

Nancy couldn't help laughing. "She is, or she couldn't be so successful in Outpatient, dealing with all kinds of problems and personalities."

"Patti's planning to move into a single soon," Shina slipped into a kimono and curled up in an enormous chair that made her look tinier than ever. "Probably the blue and white one at the end of the hall that Jonica Carr, Hamilton now, occupied. Or maybe your former apartment. We may be getting some new neighbors. I heard twin nurses had put in applications in case something opened up. If so, they may want the double apartment."

"Twins? Heaven help us if they're identical!" Nancy settled more comfortably against the couch pillows. "I trained with twins. When we did our affiliation in a hospital dealing with mentally ill patients, April was assigned to the floor directly below Allison. One day one of the patients who was close to discharge delivered clean laundry to April's ward, then went on up to Allison's.

"'Didn't I just see you downstairs?' the patient demanded.

"'No. I've been here all morning,' Allison told him.

"He turned whiter than the sink and said, 'Are you sure? I could swear I just talked with you.'

"Allison finally caught on. 'Oh, you must have talked with my twin sister. She works downstairs.'

"'Thank God,' the man fervently said. 'I thought I was seeing things and wasn't getting well after all!' "

Shina's laughter rang out. "It's funny now, but I'll bet it wasn't to that poor man. Can you imagine how he felt?"

"Not really, but then, do we ever know how others feel?" Nancy bit her lip. "Shina, something is going on at Dr. Cranston's offices." She sketched in her failure to get Damon, then his unusual insistence that she not leave the hospital.

"At least you know he isn't hurt," Shina comforted. "If he were, someone else would have answered the phone." She glanced at the clock and looked troubled. "Do you want to call again?"

Nancy's heart leapt, but she shook her head. "No. Damon will come as soon as he can. I might interrupt something important, although I can't imagine what."

They speculated for a time but came up with nothing

concrete. Time limped by more slowly than a snail with a broken foot. At last they fell silent. Nancy half-closed her eyes and observed her companion. Shina's lips drooped with unaccustomed sadness. Was it all concern for the Bartons? Or were the slender shoulders under the kimono carrying a secret, heavy burden of her own?

Shina stirred and glanced toward Nancy. The sheer unhappiness and despair in her midnight-black eyes tore at the older nurse's heart and helped push aside Nancy's own problems.

"What is it, Shina?" she asked, remembering that her friend's name stood for good, virtue. How well it fit the young woman sitting across from her.

Shina clasped her hands tightly, as if trying to hold onto her control.

"You aren't the only victim of discrimination," she whispered through unsteady lips.

Nancy's spine straightened. Her mouth dried. "You too? Oh, Shina, no!" Reared as she had been, could the gentle nurse stand up against the ugliness and danger Damon and Nancy faced?

"It isn't what you think," she explained. "No one is harassing me the way they are you." Anger flared in her face for a moment, then changed to hopelessness. She drew her silk-clad knees up and wrapped her arms around them.

"It's reverse discrimination."

Nancy had never felt more confused. "I don't understand."

Shina slowly formed the words. "Even though we live in America and I was born here, Mother and Father cling to traditional Japanese beliefs. They have no tolerance for the mixing of races. Since childhood the importance of my marrying one of my own kind has been drummed into me."

"Your own kind? But you and your family are Christians," Nancy protested.

"We are also Japanese." Shina rocked back and forth, a picture of grief.

Nancy began to understand. "Shina, have you fallen in love with someone of whom your parents won't approve? Someone who isn't Japanese?"

"I don't know."

Nancy had the feeling her friend wasn't seeing her at all.

"I don't want to pry, but if you'd like to talk about it, I'm a good listener."

"I know. I love Patti, but she—"

"—will never comprehend the reality of not being Caucasian," Nancy said.

Shina bowed her head. Her shining black hair fell around her face and hid her eyes. When she looked up again, her cheeks were wet. "From the time I first met Kevin Hyde, I sensed he was someone special. He has Irish ancestry and his name is Gaelic, meaning gentle, lovable. He's also a real Christian."

Nancy searched her memory. "I don't remember a Kevin here at the hospital."

"I met him at church." Some of the strain left her face. "We have an adult singles group. I—I felt he liked me, a lot. A few weeks later he invited me to a concert. then out to dinner. Nancy, I'm not in love with him yet, but I could be if it weren't for my parents. What should I do? Break it off? We're told to honor our father and mother." Anguish tensed her shoulders.

"Has he told you he cares?"

"Not in words." Shina's voice dropped to a whisper.

How well Nancy understood! Less than a year ago, she had seen love shining in Dr. Damon Barton's eyes, in the caress of his voice, yet for what seemed like an eternity he had spoken no words of love.

"Do your parents know about Kevin?" Nancy felt compelled to ask.

"Only that I have accepted invitations from him. I felt they had a right to know, just in case." Shina wiped the film of moisture from her eyes with a slim, tan finger. Her mouth twisted. "Even that was enough for them to start in again on the dangers of interracial marriage. Father told me this was why he objected so strongly to my living here at the hospital. He said young girls need to stay in their parents' homes where they can be watched over carefully, instead of living in apartments where they have too much freedom."

"Twenty-four isn't exactly a young girl," Nancy exclaimed.

Some of Shina's mischief returned.

"Try telling that to my father!"

The feeling Shina needed far more than she was qualified to give made Nancy ask, "Would you like to have prayer?"

"Yes."

They slipped to their knees on the soft carpet and joined hands. Shina simply asked God to guide and care for her and Kevin, for Damon, Nancy and Patti. Nancy followed, reiterating the need for wisdom in the days to come. When they rose, she felt stronger than she had since the carefree moments before she saw the assaulted white Toyota.

Shina's eyes showed she felt the same.

"Thanks. Sharing really does cut the load in half, doesn't it?"

"Yes." Nancy started to say more, but a knock at the door interrupted her. Her heart leapt to her throat and parked there.

"Who is it?" Shina called.

"Damon. Do you have a wife of mine in there?"

Nancy sprang to the door and opened it before Shina could extricate herself from the folds of her long kimono. Damon stepped inside. She searched his face for a clue to his mood. Her spirits fell.

"What happened?"

"Do you want me to leave?" Shina tactfully asked.

"No. When something like this involves anyone as well known as Dr. Cranston, there's no hiding it. Reporters will have a field day. Anyway, someone made sure the office was empty then sneaked in and trashed it." His level gaze never left his wife's face. "Same MO—err, *modus operan-di*—as with the car. Blood-red spray paint. Racial slurs. Whoever did it also dumped files and defaced paintings." Damon explained how Janet McIntyre had been lured into leaving the office. "The intruder or intruders knew he—or they—didn't have a lot of time, so he only hit the main reception area."

"Then it is you they're after," Shina said, face filled with dread.

Damon shrugged. "Looks like it. Did you have dinner, Nancy? I hope so. We have to stop at the police station so I can work with a staff artist."

He related the curious moment with the man at the deli. "They want me to come in while Auger-Eyes is still fresh in my mind."

"Nancy ate with Patti and me," Shina volunteered. "I brew good coffee and make a mean sandwich, Damon, if you can wait just a few moments."

He gave her a grateful smile and dropped to one end of the couch.

"You're an answer to prayer, Shina. I wasn't relishing a burger, but I don't want to take time for a regular restaurant." He yawned. "What a day."

Nancy gave him a quick hug, then followed Shina to the kitchenette.

"Which do you want me to do, sandwich or coffee?"

"You'll know better than I will what he wants on his sandwich." Shina's efficient hands busied themselves with the coffeemaker.

"You have enough sandwich material in here to feed an army," Nancy commented from the depths of the refrigerator. She pulled out sliced chicken breast, lettuce, tomato, onion, and condiments.

A few minutes later, Damon roused from his lethargy

enough to polish off the enormous sandwich and two cups of coffee, plus a half-dozen homemade cookies Shina had dug out of the cookie jar. When both Bartons thanked her again, she quietly replied, "That's what friends are for," and sent Nancy a look of gratitude that spoke volumes.

On the way to the police station, Nancy sat as close to her husband as the confines of her seat belt allowed. The hot coffee and food had restored some of his calmness.

"At least we know we're dealing with the same person or persons," he said. "There's one other thing. Dr. Cranston received an anonymous phone threat warning him to get rid of me."

Speechless and filled with new alarm, Nancy turned to stone.

"I volunteered to make it easy and walk out." Damon laughed. "Robert roared in no uncertain terms he didn't allow anyone to push him around."

"How can you laugh about it?" Nancy cried. "The whole thing's like a nightmare. Only it isn't just a bad dream. It's real."

"Sorry, darling." He took his hand from the wheel and squeezed hers within its warmth. "Isn't it better to laugh than to swear, or hit something?"

"I—I guess so." She wasn't convinced but kept it to herself. For the remainder of the drive, they concentrated on what they actually knew. To their amazement, the sketch artist used a computer instead of drawing a picture. Pair after pair of eyes came to the screen. Close-cropped hair in several styles. At last, Damon announced "That's him," and the artist printed out a copy.

Nancy peered over his shoulder at the stolid face, the expression in the eyes of the man in the deli. Recognition left her weak. She clutched her husband's arm. "Damon, I've seen that man. Recently. Only I don't know where."

five

Damon turned from the computer composite. "You've seen Auger-Eyes? Where? Think, Nancy."

"That's his name?" the sketch artist interrupted.

"Just what I call him," Damon admitted.

"It fits, all right."

Nancy stared at the image created from Damon's description, observing every detail—close-cropped hair, expressionless face, nondescript nose, ordinary mouth. She concentrated on the eyes. Where had she seen those eyes? A tantalizing memory hovered like a butterfly, maddeningly near but just far enough out of reach to prevent capture.

"What are you feeling right now?" the sketch artist inquired. "Sometimes identifying feelings helps a person remember." He tilted the page to one side.

Nancy turned her head to follow it. Jubilation filled her. "I have it! That man stood behind us at Anthony's Home-port in Des Moines last night. I saw his reflection in the wall mirror." Dread attacked her, the same dread she'd experienced at the restaurant.

"That's why you didn't recognize him sooner," the artist explained. "You had a reverse image because of the mirror." He looked at her keenly. "Why did you remember him at all? Did he do or say something?"

"Why didn't you mention it at the time?" Damon wanted to know.

Nancy spread her hands. "I wasn't positive if what looked like intense dislike and contempt were real or a distortion in the glass. I also wondered if he had a fetish against conceit." She looked appealingly at Damon and hot blood rose to her face. "You had just commented on what a good-looking couple we made and I'd agreed. A slight movement drew my attention to the reflection next to ours."

"You are positive it's the same man?" the sketch artist asked.

"Absolutely." She shivered. "Even when I told myself it was nothing, I felt relieved that the man who stared at us was seated at the opposite end of the room from our window table."

Within minutes, an attractive woman officer with alert eyes and a no-nonsense manner seated them in front of a cluttered desk in a small office. She closed the door and sat down across from them.

"Begin at the beginning, please."

First Damon, then Nancy, reported everything that had happened. The officer made notes, referred to the investigating officers' reports periodically and nodded when they finished. "Good. It checks."

Nancy saw a muscle twitch in Damon's jaw, a sign of inner turmoil. "Did you think it wouldn't?"

"Not at all. We just don't want to miss anything."

"Sorry." He reached for Nancy's hand. She squeezed his fingers reassuringly.

The officer's face softened into a smile. "No problem. None of us like what's going on." She paused. "We hope to identify who and maybe even why this is happening in a few minutes. We're doing a computer search with the composite to see what we have on this man. The sketch artist says you referred to him as Auger-Eyes?"

"Yes. His eyes are like shiny steel drills. When he saw me staring, they went blank."

"He did the same thing at the restaurant," Nancy choked out. Sweat formed on her palms. "It was as if he'd pulled down the blinds of a house and moved out."

"Handy trick. I may as well tell you. Doctor Barton, unless

this turns out to be one of those unexplainable coincidences, you are probably being stalked."

Nancy involuntarily gasped. Damon's fingers tightened on hers.

"I suspected as much after Nancy recognized the man in the picture." She marveled at his calm. How could he sit quietly beside her with the terrifying word *stalked* hovering in the air like a buzzard over a wounded animal?

A young officer entered and laid a printout on the desk. The policewoman nodded her thanks, dismissed him, and quickly scanned the report.

"Bingo. This guy has a rap sheet as long as your arm." Her lightning glance traveled down the page. Ummm. Not so good." She dropped the page. Her steady gaze turned from Damon to Nancy, filling the nurse with unspeakable fear.

"What is it?" Damon hoarsely asked.

"His name is Emil Schwartz, AKA Jud Marshall, Tom Elliott, and Grover Smith, depending on who you ask. He's done time for burglary, mugging, and assault. He's also an active member of a local hate group. . ."

"And?" Damon ground out.

The policewoman's face turned to granite. ". . .with suspected ties to a northwest white supremacist group."

Nancy found it difficult to breathe. She clung to her husband's hand like someone washed overboard clings to a life preserver. She couldn't have been more shocked if the investigating officer had announced they were being stalked by aliens from outer space.

"It appears he's stopped short of murder so far, if that's any comfort," she continued.

Nancy felt hysteria rising inside her. A convicted felon was stalking her husband. Now they were supposed to take comfort in the fact he hadn't killed anyone?

So far.

The grisly implication brought Nancy's spirit to its knees.

God, help us, she inwardly cried. Her mind snatched for promises, Scripture learned long ago to help her get through crises. The Bible did not fail Nancy at her moment of need. Like a geyser of fresh water springing up in the middle of an ocean came words that gave her the strength to hold on: *For [the Lord] shall give his angels charge over thee, to keep thee in all thy ways.* (Psalm 91:11, KJV)

"I know this has been a long day," the policewoman sympathetically told the Bartons. "But with this new information, I feel we need to involve the FBI. If these happenings are part of a larger plot, we're going to need them. I also want you to speak with an agent before other things crowd out original impressions, feelings, suspicions, and so on. They're usually the most accurate because you haven't had time to dissect them."

Damon glanced at Nancy, who nodded. Weary as she was, what the officer said made sense. She used the same reasoning with the nurses she directed. Items about patients that didn't get written down immediately could slip one's mind if not charted when first observed.

The FBI agent, who called himself Stone, arrived in record time. The name fit the large man. Nancy suspected he was solid muscle without an ounce of fat. She disciplined a smile, thinking Damon's Auger-Eyes nickname matched Stone even better than AKA Schwartz.

Nancy found Stone's surprisingly soft voice disconcerting. She had expected a deep rumble from the agent's massive chest cavity. He fitted spatulate fingers together.

"Now, let's see what this is all about."

Unlike the policewoman, Stone neither made notes nor referred to the police reports on the desk before him. He listened more intently than anyone she had ever known, interrupting only once to clarify a point. When he ended the interrogation—and that's what it was in spite of the agent's gentle manner—Nancy felt wrung out and hung to dry.

"I want to thank you for your cooperation and patience," Agent Stone said when they finished at last. "I also congratulate you. If more of those we interview were as observant as you two, it would make our job a whole lot easier."

He hesitated and what Nancy called a "gimlet look" sharpened Stone's gaze.

"We're going to do everything we can to nail whoever is responsible. For your sake, I hope this is simple harassment."

"It doesn't appear to be, does it?" Damon asked.

"No. If it is related to an organized group who are systematically targeting individuals and groups, we may be able to bring down some of the leaders. I can't stress how much better that would be than just nabbing the blind followers who do the actual dirty work." He stood and shook hands with each of them. "Thanks again, Doctor and Mrs. Barton. We'll be in touch."

Nancy stumbled out of the police station too numb to think.

"All I want is to go home and sleep," she told Damon when they reached their car. "I don't ever remember being so exhausted."

"Mental fatigue," he told her. "It's similar to the combat fatigue military personnel experience when pushed beyond reasonable limits." He fastened the seat belt Nancy's fumbling fingers couldn't seem to latch, then slid into the driver's seat of the Honda.

"Home, Mrs. Barton?" He put the key in the ignition.

"Home, Doctor Barton." She pressed her lips tight together, then warned him, "If you speak kindly to me one more time, I may burst into tears."

"Would you rather I ordered you to get a grip?" he teased.

It was too much for Nancy. She swayed toward him and brokenly murmured against his shoulder, "It's all so hideous. Why would anyone want to hurt you, Damon? Why?"

He held her close. "I don't know." He fell quiet, stroking her dark hair. "As long as we live in a sinful world, we will encounter those who choose evil."

Nancy had the feeling his spirit had again moved far from her. She sat up, groped in her purse for a tissue, and told him, "I know. I also know God can take care of us even in the worst circumstances." She added under her breath, *He can, but will He? God doesn't always protect those who love and serve Him.*

They reached their apartment. In spite of, or perhaps because of the stressful day, Damon and Nancy fell asleep in each other's arms, comforted by the God-given love that joined them for better and for worse. Nancy's last waking thought was how little she had known of love and real romance until she and Damon became one.

❧

Unlike the Bartons, Shina Ito did not sleep well that night. Her silken kimono wrapped her body but failed to warm her soul. Absurdly small slippers paced the rug in her softly lit apartment. They made no sound, yet echoed like heavy footsteps in her heart. She replayed her conversation with Nancy. If only speaking her doubts and uncertainties had helped her see they weren't so insurmountable as she believed! Instead, the problem loomed larger than ever.

"I'm not strong enough to go against Mother and Father," she whispered. "But how can I give up Kevin?"

Her black eyes stared unseeingly at the clock. When her legs refused to carry her across the living room even one more time, she sank to the couch. A few hours earlier, Nancy and Damon had occupied it.

Shame sent hot blood to her face. How could she be spending so much time selfishly bemoaning her own fate when her friends faced who knew what? Even now they might still be at the police station. Or driving home to their apartment, trying to hide from the terrible fears that must haunt them.

Shina slid to her knees in the same spot she'd occupied when she and Nancy prayed earlier. At first no words came. Then, a torrent. All the things on her heart and mind spilled into a great puddle before the throne of God.

Gradually peace stole over the still figure, in the same way the majestic sun crept over Mount Rainier on clear mornings. With it came the urgency to continue communicating with her Lord, but in a different way. Shina rose and went to her bedroom for a small bound notebook. Unlike those who wrote in a journal every day, the tiny nurse only wrote when she chose. Sometimes it was when she felt discouraged or especially concerned over something in her life or the lives of her friends. At other times, she wrote simply to praise God. Or to thank Him for everything from the beauty of His creation to His sending Jesus so the world might be saved from death.

Tonight, her pen raced over the pages. She wrote until she felt drained, then reread the thoughts that had poured into her journal, amazed at the content. Nothing she had written concerned her or Kevin! Instead, Nancy and Damon's needs stared back at the page, ending with the words:

> *Nancy and Damon shall be tried, but not more than they will be able to stand. God will never forsake them. One day, the glowing embers of hatred that spawns persecution will be stamped out of their lives. They will see how God's hand guided and cared for them during their most fiery trials.*

Shina felt the blood drain from her face. Was this of God, or her own thinking? What should she do about it?

"I'm not a prophet," she whispered. "Maybe this is so I can be there for them when they need me. Is it to help me keep on encouraging them if things get worse, God? It sounds as if they may."

She chilled and drew a warm afghan more closely around her. "Why would I write like this?"

A half-forgotten childhood memory teased at Shina's brain. Her grandparents had remained faithful to their many gods.

She remembered seeing pictures of the roadside shrines in Japan. Had she unknowingly been influenced by the mysticism of her ancestors? She shook her dark head. That wasn't what niggled at her. She reached for her Bible.

"Lord, what is it You'd have me know?"

She idly turned pages, but found nothing applicable. Perhaps her subject concordance would help. Beginning with A, she worked her way through the headings. Nothing seemed to fit. By the time she reached the letter P, discouragement and the need for sleep set in. Shina stubbornly refused to quit. Somewhere in the Bible was the scripture that eluded her. Patience. Peace. Perseverance. She smiled at that one. Praise. Prayer. Preaching. Prophecy.

Shina came fully awake. She read the references and went on. Prophesy. Her slim finger stopped at Acts 2, verses 17-18. She opened her Bible and read,

> In the last days, God says, I will pour out my Spirit on all people. Your sons and daughters will prophesy. . . . Even on my servants, both men and women, I will pour out my Spirit in those days, and they will prophesy. (NIV)

Again Shina repeated, "Lord, you know I am not a prophet." Yet the wheels of her mind continued turning. Had God given her insight into the Bartons' lives, as He sometimes gave doctors and nurses special knowledge? On rare occasions she had seen, even experienced, how feelings about certain cases went beyond logical explanations or test results. Each time they had proved vital to patient treatment and recovery.

"There's nothing mystical about it," Chaplain Terence once insisted during a discussion. "God works in many ways. Skilled medical personnel are trained to see and act on things others would never notice. Why shouldn't Christians also be given insight, especially if it can help save others?"

"Do I dare pass on what I wrote?" Shina wondered aloud. "God, if it's from You, I must. How do I know?"

No lightning bolt or vision came to answer her question and set her heart at ease. She switched off the living room lamps, crawled into bed, and to her own amazement, immediately fell asleep. She awakened when the alarm on her clock radio rang. Memories of the evening before rushed over her. Something in the night hours had given Shina the answer she needed. If or when God wanted her to share the sentences she had penned, He would let her know. Until then, they must remain unspoken and sacred, between the covers of her journal.

"I feel better about Kevin and me, too," she told God when she knelt for morning prayer before going to breakfast and on to work. She thought of the Christian song that talked of thinking more about others and "a little less of me." Today she would be more concerned with the needs of those around her and stop focusing so much on herself.

Shina stepped into the corridor, a slight figure in an immaculate powder blue pants uniform. She knocked on Patti's door.

"Ready?"

"Just a minute."

Patti's caroling voice tipped Shina off that the date with the pilot had gone well. So did the beaming expression above a lavender uniform that made Patti look like a bouquet of lilacs when she burst into the hall.

Shina made a droll face. "I do believe someone is in a good mood today."

"Uh-huh. We had a great time last night." Patti broke off her prattling after a few moments and sobered. "What's new with Nancy? Or did she tell you in confidence?"

"No. It will be in the papers this morning." Shina filled Patti in. "I don't know what Nancy and Damon found out at the police station. I hoped she'd call me but it probably was too late by the time they finished."

Patti turned a furious red. "It isn't fair," she choked out. "They've been through so much already. They're both wonderful and great Christians, and don't tell me God never promised us a rose garden just because we love and serve Him." She blinked uselessly long lashes.

"Slow down, Patti." Shina gave her friend a quick hug. "The rose garden's from a song, remember?" Shina thought of the words written in her journal. "God didn't promise us we wouldn't be tried. Just that He'd see it wasn't beyond our strength."

"I know." Patti's chin quivered like a hurt child's. "It's just so rotten for people to be mistreated because of their skin color. Shina, has anyone ever threatened you because you're Japanese?"

"Not threatened. A few kids in grade school made remarks, but they weren't ones I cared about, anyway." She shrugged. "There were enough of us so we didn't stand out." She held the passageway door for Patti. "I don't know how it would feel to be the only one of your ethnicity in a school."

"There aren't very many Asians at Shepherd of Love," Patti reminded her. "Employees, I mean. Does it bother you?" Her blue gaze turned to her friend.

"Here?" Shina's clear laugh rang out. "Hardly. I've never been made to feel inadequate. Except on one thing," she amended. "I'm shorter than the average nurse, if there is such a person. Someone's always teasing me about never being able to reach supplies stacked on the top shelves. That's the closest to discrimination I get at the hospital. Hey, want to hear something neat?"

"Sure." Patti's sparkle returned and she gave a little bounce just before they reached the staff dining room.

"All of our preemies are doing great and are almost ready to be released!" Shina felt a glow of happiness and satisfaction spread from her heart to her face.

"I can hardly wait to have a baby of my own," Patti confided. "Every time I see one, I think of that old nursery rhyme and fill in my own name." She chanted:

"First comes love
Then comes marriage
Then comes Patti
With a baby carriage."

"Nurse Thompson, may we have a little decorum, please?" Shina told her.

Patti smirked at her. "You can have the decorum. I want babies." She eluded Shina's outstretched hand and danced into the dining room, with her laughing friend following at a slightly more sedate pace.

six

The persecution of Damon stopped as suddenly as it had begun. Day followed uneasy day without incident. Three. Five. Seven. Ten. Yet neither Damon nor Nancy believed their troubles were over.

"It's like waiting for the other shoe to drop," Nancy burst out one evening when they took advantage of nice weather to go for a househunting drive.

"I know." Damon sounded as frustrated as his wife. He pulled the red Honda off the street to a parking space overlooking Puget Sound. The creak of swings and sounds of childish laughter from a nearby park made muted background music. The retiring sun had left its calling card, red streamers that tinted clouds and sky. Not even a whisper of breeze stirred the leaves of newly-clad trees. Damon inhaled deeply of the clean, blossom-scented air.

"If only things could always be this peaceful."

"Don't I wish." Nancy relaxed beside him. She hadn't realized until this moment how terribly tired she had grown. Not from her demanding work, but from the uncertainty of never knowing what lay just around the corner.

"It's funny we haven't heard anything from Agent Stone."

Damon stretched and laughed. "It would be funnier if we had. The FBI isn't in the habit of keeping average citizens informed of what they're doing in an investigation."

Nancy suddenly felt as bright and happy as the soft yellow dress she wore. "Well! Who says we're average citizens? We're a whole lot better than average." She cocked her shining head. "In fact, I think we're pretty special."

His dark eyes sparkled with fun. "Now that you mention it,

so do I." He glanced at his watch. "I hate to leave this spectacular sunset, but we have to get a move on or we'll be late for our appointment."

Nancy gave a little bounce of sheer exuberance. "It's hard to believe if all goes well, we may actually make an offer on a house tonight."

Damon rested his hand on hers. "You deserve it, Nancy. By the way, have I told you I couldn't have found a better woman if I'd searched the world over?"

"Only a hundred times, but never often enough." She turned her palm up, squeezed his fingers, and said in an emotion-charged voice, "I can't imagine being married to anyone in the whole world but you." With her free hand she pointed to a couple strolling along the sidewalk. "They look so young and carefree, so much in love. Yet how much more there is to real love than swinging hands and laughing together!"

"Right." Damon cleared his throat of the huskiness Nancy had learned to recognize showed the depth of her husband's feelings in tender moments such as this. He tightened his hold, then released her hand to merge into a busier street. "Now for that appointment. Are you sure you wouldn't rather have a home in one of the newer developments?"

"Oh, no." She sat up straight. "Damon, when we swung into the curving, tree-lined driveway and saw the lighted windows, it felt like the whole place was holding out open arms to me. I want to live there, to raise our children in the security of that particular neighborhood." Nancy could feel her cheeks warm.

"We shouldn't get our hopes too high," he warned. "First, we haven't even been inside. We don't know what we'll find. Maybe it needs extensive repairs. The price could also be far beyond what we've set."

"Don't be a wet blanket," Nancy told him. "Anyone who keeps a yard up the way this one's kept will make sure the interior's in excellent condition, as well. Don't ask me why, but I really believe it's our house."

"So do I," Damon sheepishly admitted. For the rest of the drive to one of the quieter outlying areas not too far from Shepherd of Love, they discussed pros and cons.

"We need to keep ourselves open so we can recognize if it isn't what God wants for us," Damon soberly concluded.

"I know. What we see as best doesn't always turn out to be God's plan." Nancy rested her head against his shoulder.

A short time later they swung into the curving driveway. The sale sign discreetly in keeping with the neighborhood swung on its chains. Nancy gave a sigh of pure bliss. God willing, that sign would soon be replaced with a sold sign. Damon opened the passenger door and she slid out, just as a shining station wagon pulled up and parked behind them. A woman with a briefcase stepped into the driveway and started toward them.

"Dr. and Mrs. Barton?"

"Yes." Damon and Nancy turned.

The woman stopped. An unreadable expression crossed her face before she slowly walked toward them.

"Is something the matter? The house hasn't sold, has it?" Nancy demanded.

"No. I mean, not exactly." She shifted her handbag under one arm.

Nancy had the feeling that for some reason the woman was waffling. The feeling that all wasn't what it should be increased when Damon sharply asked,

"Excuse me? You told me the house was definitely available when I made the appointment to view the house this evening."

Plainly flustered, the realtor glanced at the house, around the neighborhood, and back to them.

"I was just wondering how you happened to select this place. There are several developments you might prefer." She warmed to her subject. "Much more suitable for a doctor on his way up. New homes, you know."

More suitable? What was that supposed to mean? Nancy wondered.

Damon's voice turned frosty. "I believe we have an appointment to see this particular house. Shall we?" He took Nancy's arm and started up the brick walk toward the wide porch.

"Of course." The realtor sounded subdued. "I only thought—"

"I am quite aware of what you thought," Damon grimly told her.

Nancy glanced at him, puzzled by his manner. She sensed an underlying anger on his part and caught a look of almost fear in the realtor's eyes. Before she could identify the reason for either, Damon rang the doorbell. Nancy heard its chimes and the door swung open.

"Do come in. I'm Mrs. Buchanan." The white-haired, apron-clad woman's invitation was as welcoming as the hall in which she stood. Highly polished hardwood floors reflected a few well-chosen pictures on the creamy white walls. A few choice rugs broke the gleaming expanse. A graceful staircase curved upward. Nancy forgot all about undercurrents, or the need not to act too enthusiastic for fear of raising the price. She beamed at the owner.

"It's lovely."

"It is, isn't it?" A tiny worry frown between forget-me-not blue eyes erased itself and the woman beamed back. "Thank you, my dear. If you'll excuse me, I have cookies in the oven. I'll just let this lady do her job and when you've seen the house, we'll have tea." She patted Nancy's arm and trotted down the hall to an open door from which a heavenly aroma wafted.

"If you'll come this way." The realtor's colorless voice betrayed nothing. Neither did her now-bland face.

Nancy couldn't have cared less that unlike most realtors, who pointed out the desirable features of the property they showed, this one remained silent except when asked a question. The upper floor proved to be as charming as the lower. This wasn't a mere house, but a home. Nancy would wager it had seen all the births and deaths, joy and sorrow that make an older home a living personality. If they were blessed enough to buy it, she wouldn't change a thing.

"Well?" Damon whispered when the unhelpful realtor left them alone and went back downstairs. "What do you think?"

"The price is higher than we wanted to go." Nancy felt her heart must show in her eyes. "Do you think it's God's way of saying no?" She bit her lip.

"Let's wait and see. I have a hunch Mrs. Buchanan wants us to have it." His lips smiled, but it didn't reach his eyes.

Apprehension filled Nancy.

"Something's wrong, isn't it, Damon?"

"Not with the house. I like it as well as you do. We'll talk later. Okay?" He ushered her back downstairs.

"In here, please," Mrs. Buchanan called. "If you don't mind eating in the kitchen. I still have a sheet of cookies in the oven."

"Who could mind eating in a kitchen like this?" Damon told her.

"Thank you." Mrs. Buchanan cast an obviously affectionate glance around the lemon yellow and spring green decor. "You've seen the formal dining room, of course, but unless I have company, I always eat here." The visitors seated themselves at a small round table next to a plant-filled window. "It gets the morning sun."

She brought tea and a plateful of warm molasses cookies. "Help yourself. Nothing pleases me more than seeing folks enjoy what I make."

Nancy couldn't help asking, "How can you bear to leave this cozy home?"

"I couldn't, if it weren't for my family." Mrs. Buchanan crumbled a cookie. Bright mist filled her eyes. "My son's wife was killed in a car accident. Sonny and the children need me." She dabbed at her eyes with a tissue from her apron pocket. "Besides, child, home is where you're with those you love. I've been alone ever since my husband died. It will be good to be where I'm needed and loved." She chuckled. "I won't have time to get lonely in California, what with helping to raise three children, all under the age of ten."

The realtor took a swallow of tea and announced, "Perhaps we'd best get down to business. Dr. Barton? Mrs. Barton? Are you still interested?"

Mrs. Buchanan gave Nancy an astonished glance and raised her eyebrows. Did she catch the note of carefully controlled hostility the woman couldn't completely hide? If she did, she gave no sign. Mrs. Buchanan simply said, "All right. I don't want to hold you folks up too long."

Nancy shot the realtor an indignant look. What right did she have to come into this home and patronize its owner? She said nothing, but reached for another cookie and smiled at her hostess.

"I'm not going to play games with you." Damon spoke directly to Mrs. Buchanan. "We love the house. It's more than worth what you're asking, but it's also more than we can pay."

"That settles it, then." Was it satisfaction or relief on the realtor's face? She snapped her briefcase shut and stood.

"Oh, no," Mrs. Buchanan exclaimed. "Dr. Barton, how much can you pay?"

He grinned ruefully. "Five thousand dollars less than your asking price."

Shrewd blue eyes surveyed first him, then Nancy. "Are you buying with the idea of making it a rental? Or moving after a year or two?"

Nancy quietly told her, "We are buying it to be our home, for as long as God wants us to stay here."

A slow smile creased Mrs. Buchanan's face. "That's good

enough for me. I asked the Lord to let me know when the right buyers came, the ones He wanted to live here. I believe He has. I'm ready to sign, if you are." She looked around the quiet room. "It will give me pleasure, just knowing folks are living here who love the home that's been in my family since it was first built."

Now that the sale was an accomplished fact, the frosty realtor melted a bit. "The title search has already been done. As soon as you arrange financing, we can close. Mrs. Buchanan, how long do you need to remain? Thirty days?"

"I'll probably be able to leave sooner, but we'd better plan on that. It may take Sonny time to come get me." She turned to the Bartons. "If you'd like to buy some of the furniture, I'll let you have it at a good price. It's costly to transport. Besides, Sonny lives in a ranch home. It won't hold all this furniture. I just thought I'd take some of the pieces I treasure the most."

Damon and Nancy gratefully accepted. Not only would it be much less expensive than buying new furniture, Mrs. Buchanan's possessions would be more in keeping with the brick house itself. The hospitable woman invited them to come back any time they wished, to measure rooms or store some of their belongings in the basement. She patted them each on the shoulder before they left and said, "I am truly glad you're the ones."

It softened the tightness Nancy had sensed in Damon, but once in the car, she felt him tense up again.

"Are you really, truly glad?" she asked.

"Really, truly, darling." The genuineness of his smile comforted her but did not put her off.

"I still don't understand. About the realtor, I mean. The way she acted."

Damon started the engine and slowly drove out of the curving driveway. "I can't be positive, but I suspect she didn't want to show us the house."

"Why? Did she think we were lookie-loos? Good heavens, if we weren't serious about wanting the place, we wouldn't have called her!" Nancy flared.

For a second, Damon didn't reply. When he did, Nancy wondered why he had changed the subject. "Did you ever see the classic movie *Gentleman's Agreement?* Gregory Peck starred in it."

"Probably, but I don't recall much about it." Nancy tried to remember. "Is that the one where the reporter pretends to be Jewish in order to find out how serious the anti-Semitism problem is?" A cold chill went through her.

"Yes." Damon's voice sounded ragged. "He discovers that while everyone insists they aren't racist, persons of Jewish descent are barred from certain clubs and jobs. The gentleman's agreement is an unwritten, but much adhered-to pact in some exclusive neighborhoods; a promise not to sell to those who might be "less desirable," meaning anyone who isn't Caucasian."

"But that film was made years ago," Nancy protested. "With the laws about discrimination, such a practice wouldn't be tolerated now!"

Damon spoke through clenched teeth. "I know that and so does the realtor. That's why she backed off when I insisted on keeping the appointment."

"Then maybe our new neighbors won't want us." Nancy's voice trembled in spite of herself.

"I could be dead wrong," Damon admitted. "There's a chance a verbal offer was made between the time I called for the appointment and tonight. Obviously no paperwork was actually signed or the woman would have flatly refused to show us the house. Just as obvious is the fact Mrs. Buchanan knew nothing about it, if it actually happened."

"Do you think it did?" Her words came out thin and whispery.

"I suppose it could have. We'll go on the premise this

neighborhood never heard of a so-called gentleman's agreement. Remember what you said earlier, about us being pretty special? We'll give our new neighbors the chance to find out, by being friendly and setting a Christian example. Right?"

"Right," she forced herself to say. Deep inside a little voice pleaded, *Why, Lord? Just when everything seemed so wonderful, why must there be this bitter drop of doubt to take away some of the happiness?*

I'm not going to let it, she privately vowed. Better to do as Damon said and deal with the future one day at a time. Surely living an exemplary life would reap a reward of neighborhood trust and acceptance.

≈

At the same time Damon and Nancy struggled with their feelings, Shina Ito alternated between heaven and reality. She and Kevin Hyde also watched the sun set over the water, only from the window of a restaurant on the west side of Seattle. Shina knew she had never looked more charming than in the soft apricot dress she'd chosen. The look in Kevin's Irish blue eyes that went so well with his crisp, light brown hair more than rewarded her for the extra effort she had used on her hair. Shina scorned makeup, except for lipstick, but excitement had lent a rosy flush to her smooth tan skin.

All through dinner, the admiration in Kevin's face increased. When they left the restaurant, he helped her in and out of his car as though she were fragile china, easily broken. Shina couldn't help grinning behind his back when he rounded the car to slide behind the wheel. He was such a dear. If only he could see her moving furniture when the occasion demanded. Sturdy as a pine sapling, she had to admit she delighted in Kevin's treatment of her. It made her feel feminine, protected, that nothing could ever harm her.

"Shall we simply drive?" Kevin asked.

"If you like. Or we could drop in and see your family."
Shina felt a warm glow start at the tip of her small, well-

formed feet and move upward. The Hydes had accepted her as casually and completely as though she'd grown up with Kevin and his brothers and sisters. One sister, more daring than the rest, had already informed Shina she expected to be a brides- maid when the nurse married her brother.

If only—Shina gave a small sigh.

"What is it, dear?" Kevin looked at her. "Are you extra tired? I can take you home, if you like." He sounded con- cerned for her.

"Perhaps that would be best. I am tired." She didn't add her weariness came from her desire for the Itos to accept Kevin the way his family did her. How could she admit the wall of prejudice that put him out as a possible suitor for their only daughter? She ached to share the love that grew stronger every time she saw him. Pride sealed her lips. She had already seen the shadow that turned Kevin's blue eyes gray as the Irish Sea in a storm. She thought how the small sea separated Ireland from Scotland and England. Her sensitive lips twisted. Only 140 miles across at its widest point, it seemed but a trickle when compared with the sea of tradition that kept her and Kevin apart.

Just a few weeks ago Shina had told Nancy she wasn't in love with the young Boeing engineer. How wrong she had been. She realized now the strong liking she'd felt from the moment they met had gone far deeper than she knew. What could she do about it? What should she do? Where did the line begin and end between honoring parents and cleaving to the man she believed God had sent into her life? Shina twisted her hands in despair. Must she give him up in order to appease Father and Mother? If she did, she would remain single the rest of her life. No one could ever replace the strong man who sat beside her.

"Don't shut me out, Shina," Kevin told her when they reached Shepherd of Love and he parked the car near the entrance to her apartment. "I can bear anything but that."

Shina could hold back no longer. She blindly reached out for him.

"As if I could!" Hot tears fell, scorching the clasped hands between them.

Kevin's arms closed around her. His lips found hers. Shina responded with all of her newly discovered love, feeling she had sailed into a safe harbor after a long and difficult journey.

seven

"My cup runneth over," Nancy reported to Susan Devers just before their shift began on the day she and Damon would close the house deal. "I can be happy in Mrs. Buchanan's, I mean, Damon's and my house, forever."

"Forever's a long time," the LPN reminded. "How about almost forever?"

Nancy laughed and squared her shoulders under her pink uniform tunic. "If you insist. There's a large fenced back yard with flowers and trees, including a huge maple with a swing. One side is all ready for planting a vegetable garden. Mrs. Buchanan says things grow like magic. I suspect it's because she gardens with love."

Susan raised her eyebrows and a droll look came to her face. "My, my, we certainly aren't very enthusiastic, are we? By the way, just when do you and Dr. Barton intend to do all this gardening? Your schedule is already crammed."

Nancy felt the corners of her mouth turn up. "People find or make time for the things they really want to do. We'll manage."

Her friend gave a final pat to her sandy hair, washed her hands again, and asked, "I don't remember being in the neighborhood. What's it like?"

"Quieter than you'd expect for living in the city. Even though the house is old, Mrs. Buchanan had extras put in, such as double-paned windows and extra insulation. They help cut down on the noise." She debated mentioning Damon's interpretation of the realtor's coolness and decided to say nothing. They weren't sure of the reason and it would only upset the loyal LPN if she knew her friends had again

71

faced unreasonable prejudice.

"Hi-ho, off to work I go," she sang out.

"You sound like one of the Seven Dwarfs," Susan accused. Laughing, the two nurses whose work meshed like the gears of fine machinery began their rounds.

❧

That same morning, Damon also debated whether to mention to Dr. Cranston the strange experience at the Buchanan home. In a way, it seemed trivial. On the other hand, Dr. Cranston had the right to know anything that might indicate squalls ahead. The older doctor had been out of town at a medical convention for the past several days, so there had been no hurry about making a decision.

"I'll tell him," Damon resolved. Between patients, he stuck his head into his partner's office. "Got a minute?"

"Of course. Come on in."

Damon dropped into a comfortable chair in front of the cluttered desk.

"I'd like your opinion on a couple of patients." They consulted at length on the relative merits of a few more days in the hospital versus allowing the patients to go home, then Damon fell silent.

Dr. Cranston peered over his glasses. "Still worrying over the attacks?"

"No. Something else came up. It may mean nothing." Damon reported what happened at the Buchanan home.

Cranston snorted. "You think there may be an unwritten agreement about selling? I doubt it. This Mrs. Buchanan and her family have occupied the house for generations. If there's such an abomination among her neighbors, surely she'd be aware of it. From what you tell me, the woman sounds eager for you to have the place."

He fitted the tips of his fingers together and looked wise.

"Homeowners don't normally knock five thousand dollars off their asking price, especially in that vicinity. I know it well.

It's a desirable area due to neighborhood watch, excellent lighting on the streets, that kind of thing."

Damon felt a heavy load slide from his shoulders.

"Why didn't I think of that?" he asked disgustedly. "Guess your partner isn't as sharp as he thought."

The keen-eyed doctor facing him tilted his chair back and interlaced his fingers behind his head.

"We've always been open with each other, right?"

Damon nodded, but his heart pumped. Now what? Had Dr. Cranston decided to end their partnership, after all?

"I hope you won't take this personally, but there's a real danger in this for you and Nancy. I don't mean the harassment, but what it can do to you."

"I don't understand."

Bang! The chair came down with a thud.

"It's normal for you to be cautious, because of what's happened." Dr. Cranston's gaze bored into Damon. "Just don't let it make you so suspicious of everyone you end up seeing slights where they don't exist. Or take remarks personally that may have nothing to do with the fact you're an African-American." He leaned forward and spread his hands flat on a stack of folders that almost obscured his desk blotter. "Not everyone is going to like us, no matter who or what color we are."

A bubble of laughter burst from Damon's throat.

"What's so funny?" Cranston barked.

"Sorry." Damon laughed again. "I was remembering a story I heard about an old man who learned someone didn't like him. In an attempt to comfort him, his wife said, 'Don't worry so much about it. We can't expect everyone we meet to like us.'

" 'The old man exploded like a detonated bomb and shouted, 'What's not to like? What's not to like?' "

Dr. Cranston's eyes twinkled. "You just gave yourself the best advice of all. If or when you aren't sure whether it's persecution, ask yourself, 'What's not to like?' and get on with your life." He chuckled at his own wit and glanced at his watch. "Anything else? I'm lecturing at a luncheon and need to get going."

"Not a thing." Damon clasped his hands over his head in a victory signal. "Thanks."

He whistled under his breath on the way back to his office. In the interval before his next appointment, he considered what Dr. Cranston had said, recognizing wisdom and truth. It would be far too easy to unjustly accuse others of prejudice, if he or Nancy allowed themselves to become overly sensitive.

"God forbid," he muttered. "There are enough real problems to fight without attacking windmills like Don Quixote."

Damon bowed his head and earnestly asked God to help him and Nancy be free from bearing false witness against others, even mentally. More at peace than he had been for days, he allowed himself a few moments to daydream. A dozen visions came to mind: Nancy's expression when she learned the house was beyond their means. Her excitement when Mrs. Buchanan made it possible for them to purchase it. Nancy, as she would be this summer, smiling up from the rich earth in which they would dig and plant. And someday, Nancy cradling a tiny replica of him or herself, aglow with the special joy only motherhood can bring.

A sudden yearning to call her sent Damon's hand to the phone. When she answered, the lilt in her voice showed she'd had a good day.

"Are you going to be able to leave right at the end of your shift?" he inquired. "I won't really believe we're going to be homeowners until everything's finalized."

"I'll be ready," she promised.

"Good. See you soon."

A smile lingered on Damon's lips even after he broke the connection. He completed his work and went to the parking lot. Not having the white Toyota certainly made things inconvenient. Oh, well, they'd have it back in a few days. He climbed into the red Honda and headed for Shepherd of Love and Nancy.

None of the earlier frost remained in the realtor's attitude when the Bartons met her and Mrs. Buchanan to hand over a certified check. Yet Damon noticed the realtor avoided direct eye contact. Or was he falling in the trap Dr. Cranston had warned could easily snare him? His lips twitched in a grin and he murmured too low for all but his own ears, "What's not to like?" Strange how it helped. He must tell Nancy about it when they finished their business.

There had been no problem getting financing. Damon had banked with one place for years. After he married, Nancy transferred her accounts. Because current interest rates were far higher on mortgages than on savings, they chose to make a large down payment. It didn't leave much of a cushion, but they'd get by.

"We'll be happy to take you home," Damon told Mrs. Buchanan.

"I'd appreciate it, if it isn't too much out of your way. Besides, I unearthed a few more pieces of furniture you might like to see." She beamed at them, as delighted as a child with a bright red lollipop. "Will you stay for supper? It won't take any time at all to whip up a meal."

"Thanks, but why don't we treat you to dinner?" Damon courteously turned to the realtor. "You're welcome to come with us, if you like."

A wave of red crossed the prim face. "Thank you, but I really couldn't."

Again Damon wondered, glad that Mrs. Buchanan's warm acceptance drowned out the need to respond. He asked her, "Where would you like to go?"

"Anywhere that has good food," Mrs. Buchanan promptly told him. She looked wistful. "If it isn't too far, it would be nice to find a place with a view of the water. I'm going to miss that in California." She immediately made a little face. "Aren't I ungrateful, mourning the loss of Puget Sound when I'll have the whole Pacific Ocean to look at morning, noon and night!" A sweet smile brightened her countenance. "Plus the beautiful faces of my family."

Damon's gaze met Nancy's in a look of perfect understanding.

Mrs. Buchanan proved an excellent dinner companion. She drank in the view from the restaurant Damon chose, ate every morsel of her tasty salmon and pasta dinner, and expressed appreciation at being included. "If you ever come down my way, I know my son and his family will want to meet you," she told the Bartons when they delivered her at her door. "Now, come on in and I'll show you the furniture I mentioned."

The pieces proved to be a charming bedroom set, painted white and needing nothing but a good scrubbing to restore its original beauty. Damon and Nancy fell in love with it, but protested when Mrs. Buchanan insisted on practically giving it away.

"Sonny's mother wanted everything new for her children," she explained. "If you don't take it, I'll just send it to the Salvation Army for their Thrift Store. I'd much rather know people who appreciate have it. That way, it can stay with the house."

"It's perfect," Nancy exclaimed. "Thank you so much." She gave Mrs. Buchanan a spontaneous hug that was warmly returned.

All the way home, Nancy planned aloud which furniture would stay in what room and decided where to put their own pieces.

At first, Damon's enthusiasm matched her own. However, about a mile from the apartment, he noticed a dark, late model sedan close behind him. Because of the Bartons' early dinner, it was still so light few drivers had switched on their headlights. The car behind had, however. Damon changed lanes. So did the other car. He made a left turn. The sedan turned, keeping the same distance between them. Coincidence, or were they being followed? Should he mention it to Nancy? Yes. She must be prepared, just in case. In case of what? He had no answer.

In as calm a voice as he could muster, Damon said, "Don't panic and don't look back, but someone may be following us. Make sure your door is locked."

She broke off mid-sentence and went rigid beside him. Her right hand checked the door lock. "Is it all right to pull down the sun visor and act as though I'm doing my hair or makeup?"

"Fine. You can watch better than I can." His hands tightened on the steering wheel. "I'm going to make some false turns. The last thing we want to do is lead some creep to our apartment."

Nancy didn't reply. She reached a shapely hand up and adjusted the sun visor on her side. She raised one hand and pushed it through her dark hair, then dug lipstick from her purse and added it to the layer already on her mouth. From the corner of his eye, Damon caught the slight tremble of her hand, but she gave no sign she was aware of anything out of the ordinary.

A succession of turns someone going home from work or shopping might easily make confirmed Damon's suspicions. The distance between the red Honda and the dark sedan remained the same. The second car trailed like a caboose behind a long string of railroad cars. Worse, traffic had dwindled until only a few cars remained near them.

"That's it," Damon spit out. "We're heading directly for the nearest police station." He checked rearview and side mirrors, waited until the right lane was clear of traffic, and pulled over without signaling.

Bad mistake. The sedan sped up, swung sharply into the

right lane, then slowed to a crawl. Damon jammed on the brakes and stopped inches from the rear bumper of the car ahead, which immediately moved over onto the shoulder. Forehead wet with great sweat drops, he jerked the car into reverse.

A man erupted from the driver's seat of the sedan and raced toward the Honda, wildly waving his arms.

At the same time, Damon glanced behind. All clear. He stepped on the gas.

"Damon, wait!" Nancy cried.

He automatically braked again and glanced at the tall man who had reached the front of the car. Anger, relief, and nameless dread beat in his temples. He steered onto the shoulder, killed the motor, and rolled down the window.

"What are you trying to do, Damon? Lead me on a car chase all over Seattle?" Curtis Barton, a year older chronologically and twenty years older in life experience stood facing them, his mouth twisted in a cynical smile.

"So you're back," Damon ground out through nerveless lips.

"What kind of greeting is that for your long-lost brother? Especially when he comes on an errand of mercy? Hello, Nurse Nancy."

Damon thought he had freed himself from the power his brother had to hurt him. In that moment, he learned he had not. How much easier it would be if he didn't care that Curtis had aged! Marks etched by a life gone wrong and lived apart from God had coarsened a face that once looked enough like Damon's to belong to a twin. With a rush of feeling, Damon remembered how many times Curtis had traded on that likeness to escape punishment from his sins and allow his brother to take his place.

Never again. Had he spoken the words aloud? No, for neither Nancy nor Curtis showed a reaction.

"Do we have to stay here in the street?" Curtis inquired.

"Seems I remember you live not far away. That's where I was headed when I saw you." He laughed mirthlessly. "Sorry if I upset you. I could tell when you knew you were being followed. Why do good Christians like you two feel anyone would be after you?"

Damon ignored the taunt. "We'll talk at the apartment."

"Yeah." Curtis leisurely sauntered back to his sedan and drove away.

As soon as he was gone, Nancy whispered, "Did you notice his eyes when he asked about us feeling someone was after us? He looked terrified."

"I noticed." Damon started the car. "I wonder what trouble he's in this time."

"I don't know." She sounded terribly shaken. "But I'm afraid whatever it is involves us."

"How could it?" Damon raged. His hands went clammy. A knot the size of a basketball formed in his stomach. Curtis rarely showed concern for his brother. When he did, it was because his own life-style had reached out slimy tentacles and involved Damon. *Dear God, not again,* the troubled doctor silently prayed. *It was bad enough before Nancy came into my life. I can't bear it if she's put in danger again because of Curtis.*

They silently drove to the apartment, where Curtis awaited them. Damon noticed how haggard his brother looked, although he swaggered in as if he owned the place and dropped heavily to the couch.

Damon went straight to the point. "Why are you here? Where have you been since last fall? What's all this mumbo-jumbo about you coming on an errand of mercy?"

Curtis reached in his pocket for cigarettes, stuffed the pack back when Damon glared.

"Sorry. I forgot this is a no-smoking zone."

Damon's nerves screamed. "Answer my questions. What kind of trouble are you in this time?"

Anger spilled from the figure sprawled on the couch. "If you didn't always expect me to be in trouble, little brother, maybe I'd have a reason to go straight. A person might as well choose shame if he's going to get the blame. Right?" Bitterness underlined every word. "I'm in trouble, big time, but it isn't my fault."

"It never is, is it?" Damon flashed back. His brother's saw-edged laugh made Damon want to throw him out of the apartment.

Nancy spoke for the first time since they reached the apartment. "What is it, Curtis? All these months when we haven't heard from you, we've been hoping and praying you were all right."

Curtis made a small, choking sound. The anger faded from his eyes. "Thanks, Nancy. At least someone around here is willing to give me the benefit of the doubt, instead of condemning me without knowing the facts."

Damon refused to be swayed by his brother's changed attitude. Too many times in the past Curtis had played on his family's sympathy in exactly the same tone.

"Those facts would be?" he inquired in a deceptively calm voice. It successfully hid a churning stomach and the lump of lead his heart had become.

Curtis threw his head back in the proud gesture Damon knew so well. "After I left Seattle, I drifted for a time. I took a couple of jobs and—"

"Doing what?" Damon inquired sarcastically.

Curtis stiffened into defiance. "Honest jobs, believe it or not, carpentry, repair work, that kind of stuff. When they ended, I drifted to Idaho. Some of the most beautiful country in the world is there." His eyes gleamed. "Anyway, I spent the winter holed up in the mountains with what must be the last of the old-time trappers. We trapped and skinned enough to give each of us a nice little stake. I actually started believing the hard work routine might not be so bad after all."

Surely that couldn't be wishfulness in Curtis' face. Hope sprang up inside Damon. Could he have misjudged his brother because of past incidents? The words *a person might as well choose shame if he's going to get the blame* had cut deep. Was his fear of further hurt a stumbling block over which Curtis was too weak to climb? Did his brother actually care what he thought?

"What happened?" Nancy asked. Her hands lay still in her lap and her voice encouraged confidences. Never had Damon admired her control more.

Curtis stared at a wall. Damon had the feeling he was back in the wilds of Idaho.

"A piece of rotten luck. Our food was getting scarce, so my partner and I started to the nearest town to sell our pelts and restock on supplies." The wistful look grew, softening the lined, too-old-for-its-years face.

"I planned to stick with the old man until fall, at least. He said the high country in spring and summer are really worth seeing. Besides, we trapped in such an isolated area, we could make a good profit."

He smashed a fist on the arm of the couch, so hard Nancy jumped.

"If only we'd gone back the way we came in! Instead, the trapper said he'd heard of a shortcut that would save a lot of time." Curtis licked his lips. Naked pain twisted his face. "We ran into trouble."

Damon's nerves tightened until he could have walked them like a high wire. "What kind of trouble?"

Damon looked sick. "Some kind of survival group. Barbed wire fences. Men with shaved heads firing off rounds. Not rifles or pistols. Assault weapons. Heavy duty military stuff."

eight

Nancy stared at Curtis Barton. Her blood chilled until she felt ice water flowed through her veins. She braced herself, instinctively knowing there was more story to come.

Curtis's eyes glazed. His body shook.

"We discovered the hidden camp unexpectedly. I was back of my partner when we heard shots. 'Better investigate,' he told me. We peered through a pile of brush that partially screened the compound. It only took one glance to realize what was going on. Danger hung in the air like fog. The hard-faced men with their deadly target practice would never believe that of all the uninhabited miles in Idaho, we just happened to stumble on the God-forsaken place where they'd set up their survival camp.

"I couldn't move. My partner swore, then said in a fierce whisper, 'If they're white supremacists, you're dead meat, Barton. *Get out of here!*' He reached back and gave me a powerful shove. It caught me off guard. I fell, hard. Before I could get up, he marched into the open."

Nancy put her hand over her mouth to keep back a cry. She felt like a horror movie had beamed into the peaceful apartment.

Curtis wiped sweat from his forehead. His face twisted. "They didn't even ask who he was. I heard a volley of shots and a thud when his body hit the ground. I knew he was beyond any help I could give him. Something, survival instinct, I suppose, yanked me to my feet. Step by cautious step so crackling twigs wouldn't betray me, I retreated. Once out of earshot, I ran for my life."

He brokenly added, "All the time I trekked out of the

wilderness, I had time to think. If he'd been alone, the trapper would have slipped away as silently as we came. He knew if we were detected, I'd never get out alive, because of being African-American. He took a chance he could—and died in my place."

Damon quietly added, "He isn't the only one, Curtis. A man named Jesus did the same thing."

"I know." All trace of Curtis's usual mockery had vanished.

"Ironic, isn't it? I start walking the straight and narrow and this happens." He raised his head and looked deep into his brother's eyes. Nancy saw the suffering in his face. "The worst thing is, this incident may not be over. Has anything unusual happened to either of you lately? Why were you so quick to think you were being followed?"

Nancy's breathing quickened. Blood pounded in her temples. She twisted her fabric of her skirt until a thousand wrinkles appeared.

Damon sounded hoarse. "Unfortunately, yes." He reported the two incidents.

"I was afraid of that." Curtis's dark skin looked strangely pale.

"How can your stumbling on a camp in Idaho cause someone to persecute Damon?" Nancy burst out. "I don't understand. Those men didn't see you, did they? How could they know another person had been there? Or if they did, how could they identify you?"

The pupils in Curtis's eyes dwindled to pinpoints. "Hours after I escaped, I discovered my wallet was missing. I couldn't have lost it just running. It must have fallen from my pocket when my partner shoved me and I fell."

"I still don't understand," Nancy faltered. "Even if those men found it, how could they connect you to us?" Remorse filled her. "I'm sorry, Curtis. You've been through a terrible time. I don't mean to sound selfish or unconcerned about you.

I'm just trying to put it together."

"I know you are." Curtis heaved a sigh. "Even though I'm not the kind of brother Damon wants, he's all I have. The identification card in my wallet lists his name and address as the person to contact in case of emergency." He licked dry lips again and stared at the floor. "Not the apartment, the office address. Don't ask me why. Maybe a guardian angel was nudging my elbow." He grinned a crooked grin that died immediately. "I'm afraid they'll mistake him for me."

"How could they?"

"Driver's license pictures aren't the best," Curtis reminded her. "I haven't been at the address on my license for months. There's enough resemblance between my picture and Damon in person for someone who doesn't know either of us to jump to conclusions. Or they could be harassing him as a warning for me to keep my mouth shut."

Nancy caught back a little cry. Dear God, were there more and worse things lying ahead for each of them? Further taint from the evil in men's hearts?

Damon had remained silent during the recital of the Idaho tragedy. Now he sharply asked, "Did you see any of the men in the compound well enough to identify them?"

Curtis shook his head. "I don't know. It was more like a lightning glance before my partner shoved me." He closed his eyes, wrinkled his forehead, and concentrated. "They all looked alike to me, except they were different ages. Shaved heads. Army surplus clothes."

"By any chance, did one of them wear a Seattle Mariners' cap?"

Nancy's spirits skyrocketed. If only they could link Schwartz-Marshall-Elliott-Smith with the Idaho group, they would have a real clue! Hope died when Curtis regretfully shook his head.

Damon paced the floor, obviously disappointed. "Did you report to the Idaho authorities? Did they investigate?"

"Yes, but it took time to get out of the wilderness. I hung around for a few days, to find out what happened."

"And?" The word cracked like a bull whip.

"Just what we expected. By the time they got to the encampment, only the barbed wire remained. No other signs of habitation. No freshly dug grave." Curtis pressed his lips tightly together. "Not surprising. That terrain is rugged enough to dispose of a thousand bodies and leave no trace.

"There's no chance the trapper is still alive, I suppose."

Curtis mutely shook his head from side to side and Damon hastily added, "Are you willing to go with us to the FBI? If the attacks directed toward me are related, then this crosses state lines."

"That's why I'm here." Curtis gripped his brother's hand.

Nancy felt in that moment she was witnessing the resurrection of a soul. Her heart rejoiced, for both Curtis and Damon. God grant that the divine spark living inside every human being might win in its struggle to break free. She prayed the glowing embers kept alive by a brother's love would kindle. Only then could selflessness flame, reducing personal concerns to ashes in order to save another from being consumed.

A short time later, Nancy watched the flame leap to life, then settle into a banked fire of commitment, unlike anything Curtis Barton had ever shown. He admitted his checkered, unsavory past to Agent Stone when they met in his office, and followed with a crisp account of the recent happenings.

"You say you reported this to the Idaho authorities?" Stone barked, his eyes resembling twin ice cubes.

"Of course." Curtis met the unflinching gaze squarely. "The time it took me to get out gave the supremacist group time to split."

"Too bad, but it can't be helped. Thanks for coming in, Mr. Barton." He glanced from Curtis to Damon. "Your theories hold together. Whoever found your wallet would be sure to check out your last address. When you weren't there, the

next logical step was to zero in on the emergency address."
He rubbed his jaw, heavy with a day's growth of bristle. The
rasp sounded loud in the quiet room. It set Nancy's nerves
twanging.

Stone pondered for a moment, then grunted.

"We can go a couple of ways here. One is to arrange for
your so-called death, put you in the Witness Protection
Program, and have you disappear." He ignored Curtis, who
started to protest. "We can get word out on the street that you
got wasted, probably by someone you knew from the past."

"Not on your life!" Curtis leaped to his feet and shouted.
"Think I'm going to save my skin at Damon's expense?"

"Keep your voice down," Stone snapped. "You said you'd
done the disappearing act before."

Some of the old arrogance returned. Curtis sneered, "So?
That's all the more reason to hang around this time. No way
am I leaving Seattle. You might as well get that through your
thick head."

"Curtis!" Damon roared. He jumped from his chair and
grabbed his brother's arm. "Sorry, sir."

To Nancy's utter amazement, Stone laughed. It split his granite face like a crevasse on a mountainside and made him more
human. "That's what I hoped you'd say," he told Curtis. A glint
of admiration shone in his eyes. "Now if you'll sit back down,
I'll explain my second plan. It involves risk, but may pay off in
the long run."

Curtis grinned and followed orders.

Agent Stone's plan was simple.

"For the time being, do nothing," he began. "Barton, keep
away from the doctor and his wife." His head swiveled toward
Damon. "There hasn't been anything out of the ordinary at
your apartment so far, but it's highly unlikely your brother's
enemies won't learn where you live."

The words so far drummed in Nancy's ears.

"We're moving soon," Damon said.

"That's a break. Make sure your new phone number is unlisted. Between now and then, keep a close watch." Stone drummed his fingers on the desk. "How well do you know others in your apartment building?"

"Not very," Damon admitted. "Our work schedules and church activities don't allow much time for visiting."

"Good. Keep an eye out for anyone who shows undue interest in you, no matter how friendly or innocent it seems. Let me know when you're going to move. I'll make sure officers in plain clothes and unmarked cars are there to see you aren't followed to your new place." Stone hoisted himself from his chair. His eyes gleamed.

"What can I do to help?" Curtis quietly asked.

The FBI agent eyed him. "You already have. This may be just what we need to bring at least one of these hate groups down. I hope so." He ushered them out, left the door open, and headed back to his untidy, waiting desk.

❧

Nancy had long since learned the necessity of locking the door of her mind to personal problems when she donned her uniform and went on duty. The morning after Curtis's arrival, she selected the sunniest yellow outfit in her wardrobe. The color raised her spirits, although she felt bone-tired. It had taken forever for her and Damon to settle down after their exhausting session with the FBI.

Damon's eyes and smile showed how much he appreciated her efforts at cheer, but at breakfast he said, "I'd like to believe this is going to make a real difference with Curtis." He sighed. "If only he hadn't let me down so many times before. I'm afraid to hope." His mouth twisted. "I also wonder if I'm to blame."

"You?" Nancy stared across the table at her husband, scarcely able to believe her ears. "How could you be responsible?"

"I've pounded on the gates of heaven for years," Damon

quietly told her. "I've asked God to bring Curtis to his senses, *no matter what it takes*." Misery clouded Damon's black velvet eyes. "What if this is the answer?"

Nancy swallowed the lump in her throat and exploded. "Damon Barton, just what kind of God do you believe in?" She blinked back tears. "Such an answer would be like giving a stone to a child who asked his father for bread." She laid her warm hand on her husband's, strong and still on the spotless white cloth. "Curtis fell into this trouble because he was in the wrong place at the wrong time." Her voice rang clear and unwavering in the morning stillness. "That doesn't mean God can't bring good out of it. Curtis has run full speed into a stone wall; trouble so serious he can't climb over it, run away from it, or remove it from his path. I can't think of a better opportunity for God to show His power and mercy." She stopped for a breath, then rushed on.

"There's no hate group on earth powerful enough to defeat God and His purposes. So there, Dr. Barton. End of sermon number 412. Or is it 413?"

Damon squared his shoulders and threw his head back. His grim lips softened into a smile.

"Thanks, Nurse Nancy. I needed it. Now, let's talk about our new home." He kept the subject changed all the way to Shepherd of Love. Before he opened the car door to go around and let her out, Damon took both of Nancy's hands in his and looked deep into her eyes.

"I can never tell you how much you mean to me, darling." He drew her to him and tenderly kissed her.

She responded with every fiber of her being, unable to reply for the love and gratefulness surging through her.

When Damon opened her door and she stepped to the parking lot, he pressed a tiny slip of paper into her hand.

"This expresses my love far better than I can."

She started to twist it open and he grinned mischievously.

"Hold off until you're inside, okay? I'll wait."

The reminder of possible danger formed a dark cloud and marred the special moment, but Damon's reassuring smile promised protection and sent it flying. Inside the hospital, Nancy watched the red Honda out of sight before unfolding the piece of paper. All it said was: Philippians 1:3 (NIV).

Nancy clutched the message like a talisman and hurried to the chapel. Glad to find it empty, she turned the pages of the open Bible on the altar until she came to the verse she wanted. A smile started in her soul and spread outward when she read: *I thank my God every time I remember you.* What a wonderful love letter! First from Paul and Timothy to the saints at Philippi. Now from the most precious husband in all the world—and just when she most needed it. With joy in her heart and a spring to her step, Nancy carried peace from the quiet chapel with her to begin another busy day.

Patti and Shina looked relieved when Nancy joined them for lunch. She laughed at Patti's tale of a minor mishap in Outpatient and Patti blurted out, "What a relief. I was beginning to wonder if you could still laugh."

"Way to go," Shina told her. "Where's your tact?"

"Did I say something wrong?" Genuine concern shadowed Patti's blue eyes.

Nancy laughed again, feeling curiously lighthearted.

"No. I realize I've been a gob of gloom lately."

"Then things must be better. Good!" The pert blonde nurse relaxed and tackled her chef's salad with the hearty appetite that always surprised her friends.

Shina raised silky eyebrows, but Nancy shook her head. Perhaps she would talk with Shina later. Although she was just as loyal and concerned, Shina didn't tell the world her indignation the way Patti did. Patti simply could not hide her feelings when it came to one of her friends being harassed.

To Nancy's surprise, Damon sat at the nurse's station when she returned from the staff dining room.

"Hi. Why didn't you come for lunch?" she demanded,

aware of other staff members moving around them. She knew her eyes asked if something new had transpired since he left her that morning.

"Couldn't make it. Nancy, our downtown clinic and shelter wants us to admit a patient as soon as possible. It's an unusual case, but I was able to get the admission okayed. How's bed space?"

Always on top of her work, the efficient nurse had no need to check records.

"One will be available this afternoon. What's the problem?"

"A tough one. Especially for you."

A tingle of apprehension slid through her. "That would be. . .?"

Black anger mixed with pain filled Damon's eyes.

"A six-year-old boy just lost his entire family in an arson fire. The firefighters couldn't save anyone but him."

Nancy's stomach churned. "Harborview handles the severe burn cases," she reminded. "Why is he being sent here?"

"Jason has no serious injuries on the outside." Damon's lips thinned. "Inside is a whole different matter. I talked with him, actually to him, and got nowhere. I'm hoping you can."

"Because I've been there." For the space of a heartbeat Nancy relived the terrible night when she lost her mother and sister in a raging fire.

"Yes." The succinct response said it all. Damon placed his hands on her shoulders. "Others can care for this child's body. If anyone can help heal his mind and soul, it will be you, working with God."

His boundless faith in her set Nancy's lips trembling. She steadied them with an effort.

"I'll try."

She turned and beckoned to Susan Devers. The LPN had considerately busied herself a little distance away to give Nancy and Damon a bit of privacy.

"We have a new patient coming."

"The poor lamb," Susan exclaimed when Dr. Barton filled her in. "Well, we'll see he gets the best of care. If you need someone to special him, you can count on me."

"Thanks, Susan. You're a godsend." Damon smiled at her and Nancy nodded.

Nurse Devers topped all the LPNs and many of the RNs Nancy had ever supervised, both in compassion and patient care

Two hours later, Jason Street arrived without fanfare. No stretcher. No wheelchair. Just a small, silent boy with dark-chocolate face and eyes. He clung to Damon's hand, walked into Nancy Barton's ward, and straight into her heart. Jason carried a spanking new teddy bear she suspected a police officer or firefighter had given him. Just having something to cuddle and hang on to offered children a measure of security.

"Jason, this is Nurse Nancy," Damon said. "She's in charge and also my wife. Pretty, isn't she?"

A flicker of interest brightened the dull eyes, but Jason said nothing. Nancy knelt beside him and touched his hand. It felt icy. She wanted to wrap her arms around the child and never let go. So much for not allowing yourself to become attached to patients, for your own sake as well as theirs, she thought.

"I'm glad you and your bear are going to be with us," she told the little boy.

Jason looked at her with eyes that pleaded for help.

"There's someone else I want you to meet." Nancy motioned toward a bed in the far corner of the pleasant ward. "As soon as Nurse Susan knew you were coming, she fixed up a special bed for you by the window."

Again something flickered in Jason's eyes. He docilely allowed Damon and Nancy to lead him toward the cheerful corner.

"That bear of yours looks mighty tired," Susan Devers commented. "I'll bet he'd like a short nap. Not too long, though! We mustn't let him sleep too long or he will stay awake all winter when he's supposed to be sleeping, won't he?"

A wan smile crossed Jason's face. He obediently let go of Damon's hand when the doctor said, "I need to check on some of my other patients. Nurse Susan will help you into bed and then Nurse Nancy and I will be back." He forestalled possible protest by saying, "You don't have to sleep, but Teddy—you said that's his name, right?—won't take a nap if you don't lie down with him."

Nancy's heart ached at Jason's nodding head and un-questioning obedience. The track curtain closed around the new patient. Nancy heard Susan crooning a lullaby.

"Nurth Nanthy?" a childish voice piped. "Ith that boy hurted?"

She looked down at the small anxious girl who tugged at her skirt.

"He is going to be just fine," she promised. Yet the haunting memory of Jason's still face reminded her only by the grace of God and with His help could she keep that promise.

nine

Shina Ito chose Obstetrics because she loved babies. During training when she observed her first delivery, the miracle of birth filled her with the longing to be part of a team that helped bring new life into the world. Each new arrival held the same wonder that had swept through her as a student nurse. No music sounded sweeter to her keen ears than a baby's first cry.

With the coming of love, a new note had been added to the music. Shina found herself feeling part of each mother who came under her care. Would she one day be in their place, waiting for her own child, hers and Kevin Hyde's? Warm blood suffused her face at the thought. It lent her smooth cheeks such a glow, patients wondered aloud what made Shina so happy.

Today that glow vanished in the necessity for full concentration. Shina scrubbed, gloved her hands, and slipped into the sterile gown another nurse held for her. Not a trace of her usual smile turned up the corners of her lovely mouth. The patient on the table was in her mid-forties, risk enough when bearing a child. The fact it was her first complicated things further. She had gone through a difficult pregnancy, spending the last two months in bed.

Great drops of sweat formed on the patient's forehead and pallid face. Shina knew the fear in her eyes was not for herself, but for the child she had carried beneath her heart for nine long months. Thank God the husband was not only present, but able to stay calm! His encouraging voice and steady, "You can do it," mingled with the attending physician's instructions on when to push and when to relax and breathe.

Shina saw agony in the mother-to-be's face. She had stead-fastly refused any kind of pain reliever.

"I can bear it," she whispered when Shina asked her again.

"Once more. As hard as you can. We're almost there!"

A final push, a grunt of approval from the doctor, and the baby slid into her waiting hands. A small cry followed and grew into a wail.

"It's a boy," the doctor announced. "Healthy lungs, complete with all the parts in good working order!" She laughed and handed the baby to Shina, who heard the mother sob in relief. The father murmured a heartfelt, "Thank God!"

Shina held the infant up so the parents could see. She looked away from the mother's face, feeling she had unwit-tingly stumbled into a holy place.

"I'll wrap him in a sterile towel and you can hold him."

"Thank you," the father said. The exhausted mother simply held out her arms to receive her long-awaited child. Shina lin-gered long enough to see the infant snuggle into the crook of his mother's arm, then wearily followed the doctor from the delivery room.

"Gets to you, doesn't it?" the doctor softly asked while they discarded soiled gloves and surgical gowns. "I never deliver a baby without remembering Jesus."

"Neither do I." Shina's voice shook. "He left so much and came to so little."

The doctor scrubbed her hands and dried them on a fluffy towel.

"It is terrifying to consider what the world would be like if He hadn't come," she soberly said. "I don't believe I could be a physician if I didn't know God guides and directs those in our profession." She smiled. "You're a dedicated nurse, Shina. Do you plan to continue after you're married?"

"I may not marry." Shina ducked her shining black head to hide the distress she knew sprang to her face.

"That doesn't seem possible," the doctor commented. She

glanced at the large wall clock. "Uh-oh. I have to run. Thanks again." She breezed out, leaving Shina to stare blindly and wash her hands over and over.

Tests used to discover possible problems in newborns showed the latest arrival to be normal and healthy. Unlike some hospitals, Shepherd of Love kept mother and baby a minimum of three days, longer when necessary. On the fourth day, the ecstatic father came for his family. The nurse smilingly told them good-bye, feeling wistful. If only she. . .Shina couldn't finish. How did one fight tradition and break chains forged by the past?

She asked Kevin the same question that evening, leaning against the rail of the ferry boat coming home from Vashon Island, one of Shina's favorite outings. Unlike heavily populated Seattle and Tacoma, the island offered peace and quiet, with tree-lined roads, small farms, and gorgeous views of Puget Sound.

"Could you be happy living in a place like this?" Kevin huskily asked. He put his hands on Shina's shoulders and turned her toward him. "With a hard-working, upstanding guy like me, for instance?"

Something about the lovely evening made Shina throw caution to the winds.

"I think I could be happy with you no matter where we lived. But I'm not so sure I'd want to be in a place accessible only by water or air."

He pulled her toward him until her head nestled against his steadily beating heart.

"There's talk of building a bridge to Vashon."

Shina shook her head vigorously. "That would ruin it. The island's main charm is its lack of people." She fell silent, content just to be with him. "Kevin, what are we going to do about my parents? How can we convince them our love is real, and a gift from God?"

"I've been giving it a lot of thought," he told her.

She glanced up. His Irish eyes looked more gray than blue. Breeze from the Sound had ruffled his crisp, light brown hair until he resembled a small boy.

"I think it's a mistake not to let your parents know how we feel," Kevin quietly said. "Even if they don't approve, I believe if I go to your father and formally ask permission to marry his daughter, it will show my intentions are honorable." The twinkle in his eye and quick laugh did not quite hide Kevin's awareness of how serious the problem really was.

Shina had never loved him more.

"It's worth a try. I can't think of anything else."

She pressed her head back against Kevin's chest and felt his hand stroke her hair in a rhythmic motion.

If I could only stay in his arms forever, she passionately thought. *How can I give him up, God? Yet how can I show dishonor to my parents, if Father will not listen and give us his blessing?*

"Is it proper for me to approach him alone?" Kevin wanted to know. His laugh rang out across the water, but didn't hide the note of anxiety. "I've never pleaded with a father for his daughter's hand before."

Shina tried to match his mood. "You won't have to again," she teased.

"I hope not!" he fervently agreed. Tipping her chin up, he gazed into her face.

"If we marry, you know you're stuck with me, don't you? For better, for worse, the whole thing. Divorce is not a word in my vocabulary."

"As if you had to tell me that," she scoffed. "Believe me, Mr. Irish Kevin Hyde, once we say 'I do,' I'll hang onto you for life."

She stood on tiptoe and pressed her lips to his, recognizing how precious the moment was and tucking it away in her heart. Someday when they faced storms, they would take out the memory of this pearl-tinted evening and find peace by reliving it together.

"You haven't answered my question," Kevin reminded. "Do I ask for an audience with your father? Should you be present? Your mother?"

"Oh, no," she quickly assured him. "Tradition says this is man to man."

Kevin proudly raised his head. "I'll call him when we get home and ask him to set a time for me to speak with him."

An awful thought crossed Shina's mind. What if Father refused? Yet, why should he? Although he knew she had been seeing Kevin, at this point he could not know the only daughter of the house of Ito was considering marrying a Caucasian. Why must skin color divide, even among Christians? It wasn't as though she and Kevin were lovestruck teenagers.

"I'll be praying," she choked out.

His arms tightened around her. "So will I. Remember, Jesus said that where two agree, our Father in heaven will do what they ask. [Matthew 18:19] We do have to make sure to ask if it be in His will."

Shina nodded and confessed, "That's the hard part. When we feel so strongly our love is right, it isn't easy to admit that just maybe God doesn't see it so."

"We'll pray He does," Kevin added. "Time to get back to the car. The ferry is about to dock."

Dinner at a seafood restaurant near the ferry terminal on the mainland and a contented drive home offered an interlude between dreams and reality. Back in Shina's attractive apartment, Kevin strongly punched in the telephone number of the elder Itos. Shina held her breath, listening to see if his tone of voice would indicate a favorable climate.

"Hello, Mr. Ito. This is Kevin Hyde." He took a deep breath. "I would appreciate the opportunity to speak with you, Mr. Ito. Would you be free one late afternoon or evening this week? . . . Yes, it's about Shina . . . No, she is fine . . .

"Tomorrow at 5:30? . . . Excuse me? You want me to bring

Shina? Of course." Relief surged into his face. "Thank you, Mr. Ito." He slowly cradled the phone and licked dry lips. "He asked me to be very sure you come with me."

Shina's muscles twitched. "How odd."

"Is it likely to be a good sign?"

"I don't know," she frankly admitted. "I dislike clichés, but the expression *poker face* fits my father. When he doesn't want others to know what he's thinking, he adjusts his face until it looks masklike." She shook her head. "Tomorrow night should be ver-r-r-y inter-r-resting."

Her attempt at lightening the conversation brought a full-bodied response. Kevin doubled over with laughter. "Anyone who can roll their R's that way is already half-Irish." He paused. "I just wish I knew how to get across to your parents, especially your father, how much I love and want to take care of you. I'm proud of your Japanese-American heritage."

"I know you are. That's one of the things I love most about you." Shina knew her eyes mirrored the innermost parts of her soul when she looked up at Kevin.

Before he left, they knelt, joined hands, and poured out their desires to God, making sure not to dictate, but to simply place the matter in His care. Shina felt strangely comforted. Peace and the memory of Kevin's goodnight kiss lingered long after he had gone.

An unusually heavy work schedule the next day left scant time for personal reflections. Shina grinned, remembering the old saying about idle hands finding mischief. Her small but capable ones certainly had no time for mischief today! Two morning deliveries made her late to lunch. She reached the staff dining room just before they closed, a little relieved she'd missed Patti and Nancy. Alone at the table, she took time to think of the upcoming interview. Her tasty lunch turned to sawdust in her mouth. Shina pushed it away, half-eaten. What would her father say when he learned how serious she and Kevin had grown?

An equally demanding afternoon mercifully saved her from more speculation. Shina wearily reached her apartment and stretched out on the sofa, too tired to think, knowing she must.

"We really need Your help, Lord," she prayed.

Waves of fatigue broke over her. She closed her eyes, willing herself to relax. After a few moments, she sat up and reached for her well-worn King James Bible. Memory of a specific verse tantalized her, one that could be important in this time of need.

Shina concentrated—hard. She quickly turned to 1 Corinthians, 12:12-13 and read,

> *For the body is one, and hath many members,*
> *and all the members of that one body, being many,*
> *are one body, so also is Christ. For by one Spirit*
> *are we all baptized into one body, whether we be*
> *Jews or Gentiles, whether we be bond or free; and*
> *have been all made to drink into one Spirit.*

Shina's heart leapt. She sprang from the sofa and took out a New International Version. She read,

> *The body is a unit, though it is made up of many*
> *parts; and though all its parts are many, they form*
> *one body. So it is with Christ. For we were all bap-*
> *tized by one Spirit into one body—whether Jews or*
> *Greeks, slave or free—and we were all given the*
> *one Spirit to drink.*

"Thank You, Lord," Shina whispered. Rejuvenated by the words the Apostle Paul gave to the church in Corinth centuries before, Shina carefully copied the Scripture and lay aside her fatigue. A quick shower, a cherry-red skirt and the white blouse Kevin particularly liked made her ready and waiting.

Her stomach growled, reminding her of her half-eaten lunch. Shina's laugh trilled out.

"How unromantic! Heroines in novels are supposed to live on love and love alone."

She grabbed a banana and a glass of milk to appease her protesting stomach. She and Kevin planned to go out for dinner when they left the Itos.

"I know we would be welcome to stay," Shina told the quiet room. "It just might not be comfortable. It all depends on Father."

Again she felt like a wishbone, pulled two ways. If she were forced to choose between Kevin and her family, what would she do?

"I don't honestly know," she whispered. An insistent *oh, yeah?* pounded in her ears, drowned out only by another prayer for help, guidance, and above all, strength and wisdom.

"Thanks for wearing that outfit. You look great," Kevin told her when she opened the door and held out her arms to him. He gave her a quick hug and dropped a kiss on her lips.

Tingling from his nearness, she pulled back and surveyed him. His gray suit set off both his light brown hair and blue-gray eyes. His face looked tan above a pale blue shirt and blended blue and gray tie.

"So do you—like you just came from the dry cleaners."

One eyebrow quirked and gave him a droll expression. "As in stuffed shirt?"

"Of course not." Shina laughed and felt tension melt away. She handed him the Scripture she had copied earlier.

"I found some ammunition for you." One hand flew to her mouth. What a stupid thing to say, as if they were rushing headfirst into a war zone!

"I hope there won't be a battle," he told her. A poignant light grayed his eyes and he admitted, "I have to confess, I've been mustering everything I could to convince your father. What is this?"

"Just read it." She slipped away to her bedroom and caught up a lightweight white sweater. In case they later decided to walk, she would need it. Breezes from the Sound often carried chill, along with the tang of salt.

That same chill dampened Shina's spirits when she and Kevin reached the Ito home. Her father wore the mask she had described the other night. Both he and Shina's mother showed faultless courtesy, which didn't warm the atmosphere. Mrs. Ito immediately brought tea and tiny cookies to the large living room that combined Japanese and western decor. Shina caught Kevin's admiring look at the Oriental rugs on the hardwood floor, the ornamental fan on the wall above the television set, silk paintings of snow-capped Mt. Fujiyama and Mt. Rainier on opposite walls, a picture of Christ above the mantel. If only the two cultures could blend equally in her father's mind!

"You wished to see me?" Mr. Ito said when the tea ceremony ended. "You said it has to do with my daughter. I see she is well, so perhaps your coming to me involves matters of the heart." Not a quiver betrayed whatever emotions he might conceal beneath his crisp white shirt and well-cut sports jacket.

Shina gasped. She hadn't expected her father to begin like this. She looked into his inscrutable face and her heart sank to her toes. Kevin obviously could expect no help in the coming interview.

"Father—"

He cut her short. "I asked both of you to come, because there are things I must say that you each need to hear. So does your mother. But it is for the young man and your father to do the speaking."

Habits of a lifetime forced Shina to nod and lower her head. Antagonizing Father by demanding the right to be heard could hurt any chance of receiving her parents' blessing. She sent a pleading look toward her mother, an older edition of herself who sat with folded hands in the lap of her navy blue dress.

Mrs. Ito's tremulous smile comforted but did not help Shina. Father was and always had been head of the household. If Mother secretly took him to task or disagreed concerning some family matter, it would be in the privacy of their room. Steeped in tradition, Mother would find it unseemly to openly question her husband, even though many of their friends' wives spoke freely.

Shina could not blame her mother. It had taken all her own courage simply to convince Father she should live at the hospital. The discussion had raged for weeks. He finally consented only when she reminded him of the long distances she must travel from home to work, and how difficult it was in bad weather.

Kevin's voice snapped Shina to attention. He leaned forward in his chair and said, "Mr. Ito, I did not plan to blurt it out this way, but I love your daughter. Although it is hard to believe, she also loves me." A look of wonder brightened his eyes. "I want to love and cherish and protect her for as long as she lives. I ask for your daughter's hand in marriage."

The older man fitted his fingertips together and allowed a full minute to pass while Shina's nerves screamed. At last he spoke. His measured tones sounded a death knell to the young couple's hopes. "I appreciate your candor and forthrightness, Mr. Hyde. However, I do not feel it is good for persons of different races to marry. My daughter can only find true happiness by marrying one of her own kind."

Red stains covered Kevin's tanned face. "I respect your beliefs, sir. I also disagree with them. As Christians, we are no longer Jews or Greek, slave or free, but one in Christ. I am Shina's kind, as she is mine. My family has welcomed her as another daughter and sister."

Mr. Ito's mask slipped. His voice changed to cutting steel. "Ah. Then you have told others of your intentions before speaking with the father of the woman you wish to marry."

Kevin flung his head up proudly. "We have not. They fell in love with Shina the first time they met her, as did I. Never by word or deed have we indicated we hope to marry." A boyish grin relieved his seriousness. "I admit they have not been so reticent! I believe they knew I cared, before I did. At least, they have dropped enough hints one would have to be deaf to ignore their hopes."

Mr. Ito said nothing, but his fathomless gaze turned toward Shina. "Is this true? Do you love this young man?"

She raised her head and looked straight into his face. "More than life itself."

"If I do not consent, will you marry without my blessing?"

The moment she had dreaded with all her heart had arrived. Shina searched herself, seeking an answer to her father's—and her own—question. The unhappiness in Kevin's face lent strength. She left her chair, crossed to her father, and knelt beside him. She laid her hand over his, noting the parchment-like quality. She had been born late in her parents' life. She knew it contributed much to their protectiveness.

"What kind of love asks such a cruel question?"

"The love of a father who longs for his only child's happiness."

"I have been your faithful daughter, Father. Now I am no longer a child. I am a woman, with a woman's heart. Withholding your blessing means forcing me to choose between you." Hot tears fell. "Will you do that to me?"

For a long time, Mr. Ito did not reply. When he did, it was to say, "We shall speak no more of this now." He rose, shook hands with Kevin, and smiled for the first time that evening. "I promise to think of all you have said."

Shina didn't dare ask how long it would take. The fact Father hadn't insisted on an answer tonight offered a dim ray of hope. Would he be able to change the thinking of a lifetime? If not, how could she marry Kevin without bringing pain? And in her father's eyes, dishonoring him and her mother?

ten

For three days in a row, Nancy and Damon arrived home to find a mystery. Each afternoon, they discovered a floral bouquet had been delivered to their apartment. None of them bore a card. None had an identifying tag to show the name of the florist shop.

Damon checked them thoroughly, to make sure no bugging device had been cleverly inserted. He found nothing, but remained suspicious. He promptly took them to the dumpster and both he and Nancy scrubbed their hands thoroughly, in case some harmful substance had been added. After the third delivery, Damon reported the deliveries to Agent Stone.

The FBI man grunted and promised to check it out. Two hours later he called and ordered Damon and Nancy to come to his office that evening. To their amazement, Curtis Barton was already there when they were ushered inside.

The door closed. Stone announced, "Against direct orders, your brother decided to take things into his own hands. If it happens again, I'll throw the book at him." Disapproval oozed from every line of Stone's rigid body. He rubbed his hand over his face in the rasping sound that set Nancy's teeth on edge.

"What have you done this time?" Damon demanded.

Curtis put on an innocent expression. "Discovered someone's watching your apartment building."

"We already knew that," Stone put in. His mouth puckered and he looked like he'd been sucking lemons.

Nancy swallowed back the fear that threatened to choke her. She reached for Damon's strong hand.

"How did you find out?" he asked Curtis. A sheen of sweat filmed his face.

Curtis raised an eyebrow. "No big deal, man. Who's going to suspect the driver of a florist van?"

"You delivered the flowers? Where did you get the van? Steal it?"

"No way. I called in a favor from a guy I helped once. He did time, then went legit. Owns his own flower shop. I told him I needed a job. I've been delivering pretty little posies. Did you like yours?" Curtis grinned, clasped his hands behind his head, and tilted his chair back on its hind legs. He resembled Damon more than ever when he smiled.

"Like I said, no one pays attention to flower vans. Seattle has dozens of them. Pretty good excuse to be in the neighborhood and keep an eye out for suspicious characters, right?"

"You never once considered anyone watching might recognize you?" Stone said sarcastically.

"Why should they?" Curtis looked honestly surprised. "I wore a fake mustache and beard, and combed my hair down over my eyes. I doubt even Damon would have recognized me. I also made sure no unusual-looking persons were around when I got out of the van and went into the building." His eyes glittered. "It worked, too. I saw your friend in the baseball cap."

"Schwartz whatever his name is? When?" Damon stared at his brother. Nancy straightened as if ice water had been dumped down her back.

"This afternoon. He was in a parked car across the street just before you came home. A patrol car halted at a four-way stop. Schwartz took off, real slow and easy, not to attract attention. He wasn't there when you arrived."

Nancy gasped. Damon's face turned to granite.

"Don't show up there again," he commanded.

An unreadable expression flitted across Curtis's face. Wishfulness? Longing to have his efforts on their behalf recognized?

He quietly said, "I won't have to, will I? Stone's men have

the license number of Schwartz's pickup."

The FBI agent's big fist crashed to the desk. "I'm warning you, Barton. One more stupid move like this and I'll nab you."

Curtis let his front chair legs come down with a bang. His mouth slitted until it seemed impossible words could come out.

"Damon is my brother, Stone. I got him into this, although God knows it wasn't my fault—this time."

Nancy thrilled at the love and regret in Curtis's voice. Damon's convulsive grip of her hand showed how much it meant to him.

Stone didn't budge. "If you really want to help your brother and his wife, let me handle this. My way, in my time. Got it?"

Curtis grinned a crooked grin that didn't reach his eyes. "Yeah. Sure you don't want to swear me in as a special deputy or something?"

Nancy thought Stone would explode. He bit off something she suspected was more profane than polite, then thundered, "Don't hold your breath. Now get out of here. No, wait." He fitted his fingers together speculatively. "Barton, keep that job with the florist. It might just prove useful. But stay away from the apartment building. Or in the words of the old-time western sheriffs, I'll nail your hide to the barn door."

Curtis sobered. "Can't blame you for that. I'd do the same in your place."

He followed Nancy and Damon out of the office, but held a powerful arm in front of them when they reached the door to the parking lot.

"I'll go first." He stepped outside, scanned the deserted area, and motioned. "All clear." Yet Curtis did not start toward his own car until he saw them safe in the red Honda.

"Don't think I don't appreciate what you're trying to do," Damon quietly said.

A flash of gratitude brightened Curtis's somber face.

"Thanks." He shifted from one foot to another. "Uh, I've

been doing a lot of thinking about what you said. You know. That the trapper was the second one who died to save my skin. I have to admit it makes a lot of sense." He wheeled as if ashamed of the confession, lightly ran to his car, and slid into the driver's seat. He beckoned for them to precede him and after a few blocks turned in the opposite direction. The last they saw of him was one hand held up in a victory signal.

"I doubt either of us will ever know what it cost Curtis to say what he just did," Damon told Nancy on the way home. His voice was so husky she had to lean closer to hear him. "Nancy, except for what this is doing to you, I would thank God for everything, if Curtis only surrenders his life to Christ. Why must innocent persons be hurt by the sins of others? It seems you will never be free from the effects of the life my brother chose apart from God!"

She laid her hand on his arm and confessed, "I have asked myself—and God—that very question a million times."

"Have you received an answer?" he asked in despair.

"Yes. In 1 Peter 4:12-13. 'Beloved, think it not strange concerning the fiery trial which is to try you, as though some strange thing happened unto you: But rejoice, inasmuch as ye are partakers of Christ's sufferings; that when His glory shall be revealed, ye may be glad also with exceeding joy' (KJV).

"Don't you see?" She tightened her hold on his arm. "Persecution and evil may win a skirmish, even a battle. They can never win the war! God will eventually triumph. So will we." She took a deep breath and released it. "When we married, we became one, Damon. Curtis is my brother now, as well as yours. He is not the same man he was before the Idaho incident. Seeing him tonight was like watching a tightly folded bud slowly begin to unfurl in sunlight." She fell silent for a moment.

"I have the feeling Curtis is being strengthened by the Holy Spirit for the time when he must choose forever between the darkness and the light. I believe he will be able to take his stand for Christ."

"If only it is true!" Damon cried out.

Discernment Nancy hadn't known she possessed opened her mind and eased the heart that ached for her husband.

"Perhaps the greatest gift we can give Curtis is to believe in him," she softly said. "I know it won't be easy. It never is when those we love have betrayed our trust again and again. Our prayers must be not only for Curtis, but for ourselves, my darling."

Damon did not reply, but she felt the knotted muscles in his arm relax beneath her hand. That night he fell asleep in Nancy's arms, head cradled on her breast, like a weary child who has sought and found comfort from one who loves him without reservation. She remained awake for a time, thanking God for the love of this strong man. His only weakness lay in his depth of caring for a prodigal brother.

⁂

The challenge of restoring Jason Street's mental and emotional health helped keep Nancy from brooding too much on her own circumstances. Damon reminded her in vain how unwise it was to become attached. She agreed wholeheartedly, then acknowledged the warning had come too late. From the first moment she saw Jason, the similarities of their childhood created a bond. It grew with the speed of light when he slowly began to respond to her. It also created havoc in her mind. Always conscientious, Nancy found herself resenting the time she spent away from Jason in order to accomplish her other work and not neglect the rest of her patients.

She could not pinpoint the moment when the idea first started to haunt her. Nancy immediately discarded it as impractical, unbelievable, impossible. The idea returned sevenfold, seven hundredfold, hammering at the gate of reason and the heart she desperately attempted to bar.

One afternoon she found Jason sobbing, face in his pillow as if ashamed to have those around him hear. Nancy pulled the privacy curtain, gathered both him and his bear into her arms, and spoke into his ear.

"It's okay to cry, Jason. God gave us tears so we can get rid of our sadness and feel better. I'm here."

He buried his face in her peach uniform tunic and let the hot tears come. She rocked him back and forth until he sagged against her in sheer exhaustion.

With a quick prayer for guidance, Nancy whispered, "I know how badly you feel. A long time ago, my mother and sister died in a fire, just like your family." She felt a ripple of movement. He raised drenched dark eyes to hers. A small brown hand reached up and stroked her face. A broken voice said,

"It's okay to cry, Nurse Nancy. I'm here."

The sad voice brought bright drops. One splashed on Jason's comforting hand. He continued to pat her cheek, tracing the drop as it fell. After a long time, she raised her head and said, "My goodness, I'm all wet."

Jason laughed, for the first time since he came to Shepherd of Love.

"All wet," he parroted. "Nurse Nancy's all wet."

Nancy took tissues from her pocket and dried their tears. She laid Jason back against the pillow and smoothed Teddy's rumpled fur. She brought a basin and washed Jason's hot face.

"Sleep, dearest," she told him. "When you wake up, Nurse Susan will bring you some ice cream."

"Will you come, too?" Fear chased mirth from his expressive eyes.

"Of course." Nancy sang a low lullaby until Jason's eyelashes made half moons on his dark-chocolate cheeks. Clutching Teddy, he slept the most peaceful sleep he had known since the terrible fire.

Later that afternoon Susan came to where Nancy was checking charts. The LPN's motherly face wore an expression of concern.

"Jason wants to see you, but before you go, there's something you need to know." She looked apprehensive and bit her lip. "When he woke up and I gave him his treat, he asked me some pretty serious questions."

"Questions?" Nancy put down her pen.

Susan's steady eyes looked straight into hers.

"Yes. Jason is one smart kid, Nancy. He said, 'Dr. Barton and Nurse Nancy like children, don't they?' I told him you did. He knows you and Dr. Barton are married, of course. He wanted to know if you had any children. I told him no, not yet." Susan wrung her hands and her supervisor stiffened, dreading what she instinctively felt coming.

"Nancy, Jason thought it over and then asked, 'Do you think they might want a little boy like me?' " Susan's eyes overflowed. "It just about broke my heart."

Nancy felt the blood drain from her face. "What did you say?"

Susan dabbed at her eyes. "What could I say? I mumbled something about us not being able to get along without him here, and walked off before I blubbered all over the place. What are we going to do?"

A tumult of protest against Jason having to face a world bereft of real love tore through Nancy. It crystallized feelings she had forced herself to ignore but could no longer deny. Knuckles white from clenching the edge of the desk, she proudly flung her head back and said for Susan's ears alone, "God and Damon willing, I am going to adopt Jason."

Susan's hand flew to her mouth to stifle a glad cry. Her face lit up like downtown Seattle in December.

"Do you mean it?"

"With all my heart," Nancy replied.

The LPN's excitement vanished. A look of dismay crossed her face.

"Will Dr. Barton agree? I mean, with everything that's been going on in your lives lately. . ." Her voice thinned and faded.

Nancy fell from the pinnacle of happiness into a bottomless pit of despair. She wordlessly stared at her friend, mind whirling. Even if Damon were willing, they could not adopt Jason. No judge in his or her right mind would award a child to a couple in their present situation. Even more important, she and Damon dared not bring Jason into possible danger.

Rebellion surged through her.

"We're going to get to the bottom of this," she promised in a low, ragged voice. "Surely God won't allow hatemongers to control our lives, or Jason's."

Susan patted Nancy's shoulder.

"I'll be praying, too," she whispered, then swung down the ward in her unhurried way to answer the fretful summons of one of their small charges.

Nancy fled to the staff rest room, bathed her flushed face, and did some deep breathing to regain control. Children keenly sensed turmoil in those who cared for them. They didn't need her problems to compound their own. With a quick prayer for help, she dredged up a smile and went back on duty.

Fleeting glances showed that Jason alternated between looking out the window and watching her as she worked her way toward him. The unconscious pleading in his eyes made her more determined than ever to help in whatever way God permitted. Yet even though part of her attention focused on the small boy, Nurse Nancy did not neglect the others.

Each child had something to share: a floppy cloth doll, a favorite stuffed toy, news that Dr. Barton had said they could go home soon. Proud boasts from those who had learned to wiggle their ears, or had taken a few more steps for the physical therapist. Laughter from those on the mend; feeble smiles that tore at her heart from the two sicker children in a semi-private room. She lingered with them, taking time to encourage and pray.

At last she reached Jason.

"Hello, again. Nurse Susan tells me you ate every bite of your ice cream. Woops! You missed your mouth once." She expertly removed a milky stain from his chin and gave him a big hug.

His arms closed around her, surprisingly strong in spite of how skinny they were.

"Who will take care of me?" he blurted out.

She felt a ripple of shock flow through her, knowing Jason was really asking for a commitment of love she could not give, at least not yet. She pretended to misunderstand.

"What? Aren't Nurse Susan, the other nurses, and I taking care of you? My goodness, Jason, I thought we'd been doing a good job."

"When I go away," he said. One tear slipped down his satiny cheek.

Nancy knelt by his chair. "We're going to keep you here as long as we can," she told him. "We love you and we'd miss you if you left us."

"I want my mama," Jason whimpered.

Nancy looked up to see Susan considerately pulling the privacy curtain, face red as fire with her struggle to hold back her feelings.

"I want my mama, too," she said quietly. "But she's gone to live with Jesus."

Interest stirred in the dark eyes. "In heaven? That's where Daddy and Mama said people who love Jesus go."

A flood of relief threatened to swamp Nancy. Thank God this child came from a Christian home! It made it so much easier to deal with heartbreak when she could offer the assurance of meeting again.

"Yes, dear. Do you know what? I'll bet your family and mine are already acquainted."

"I wish I could go, too," came the wistful reply.

"Someday you will," Nancy promised. Her voice rang with truth. "First, Jesus wants you to grow up and make Him and your family proud of you."

Jason's eyelids drooped from mental fatigue.

Nancy talked in a low monotone, describing the many things he might be. Soon Jason slept, but Nancy could not forget the forlorn expression in his troubled face when he wanted his mama. Or the haunting echo of his childish cry, *who will take care of me?* What hurt most was the knowledge Jason did not cry alone. Thousands, no, millions of children around the world daily raised their cries for help. *How long, Lord, must those cries go unanswered?*

Jason was lucky to live in a country where he would receive basic care. Yet Nancy shrank from the bleakness he might well face. Too many couples willing to adopt wanted babies, not six-year-olds. There were not enough African-American adoptive families to handle all the available children of their own ethnic origin. Controversy raged concerning the practice of Caucasians raising African-American children, although some provided all the love and care every child needed. Foster care ranged from excellent to inadequate. Many times short-term placements meant children were transferred from home to home during their most formative years.

Must Jason suffer a mushroom existence, the rootless feeling that he belonged to no one? Would the faith in Jesus his parents had so carefully instilled in him be strong enough to keep him safe and strong? Nancy shuddered. That faith needed to be carefully nurtured. Unless Jason were fortunate enough to be placed in a Christian home with those who role-modeled Christ, what chance had he of clinging to his early teachings?

She thought of various studies, the incontrovertible evidence showing how much danger lurked ahead for children shoved from one foster home to another. Children raised without continuity and exposed to different rules and standards in each place they lived grew confused and insecure far too often. Statistics showed their increased risk for everything from rebellion to trouble with the law. How many children and teens ended up in trouble simply because they needed to belong—and became easy marks when offered entrance into gang or cult.

Nancy looked down at the sleeping child, innocent, trusting. *I will not allow Jason to become a statistic, or fall through the cracks of the system,* Nancy silently vowed. She picked up Teddy, who had slid from Jason's lax hand to lie on the floor and look up at her with accusing eyes. She put him next to the small boy's face. Jason stirred slightly. His hand closed on the stuffed bear that meant security; the one thing he believed would not be torn from him when everything he loved had been taken.

Nancy turned away, sick at heart. Despite her vow, her determination to save this child, what hope had she of accomplishing it? Her lodestar verse, Philippians 4:13, crept into her soul and brought a measure of solace. *I can do all things through Christ which strengtheneth me.* Surely God would make a way through the darkness that surrounded her and Damon and prevented them from rescuing Jason.

eleven

An uneasy stillness greeted Dr. Damon Barton outside the rear door of the apartment building he and Nancy were vacating in the dead of the night. A moment later, the muted wail of sirens broke the silence. Damon glanced around him. A few parked cars across the street appeared vacant. His heart pounded. *Appeared* was the operative word. At least three of those cars held plainclothes officers, crouched low and waiting in case of trouble. Somewhere down the block, a motor sprang to life. Coming toward him were headlights made sickly yellow from the dense fog that rolled in off Puget Sound.

Damon automatically stepped back and peered through the gloom. He had taken the precaution earlier of disconnecting the light above the back door. Hidden by the fantastic shadows cast by streetlights dimmed by the fog, he tensed and stared at the approaching vehicle. Friend or foe? Moving van or a plant? A dog howled, raising the hair on the back of Damon's neck. A sickening feeling of déjà vu swept through him. Why? He had never before huddled in a doorway while an unknown quantity approached.

He tried to laugh off his apprehension. The ominous night had evidently triggered half-forgotten stories from childhood. His breath quickened and his chest constricted. For a moment he was one with his slave ancestors, terrified but determined to escape the enemies who hounded them. The dog bayed again. Damon shuddered. Cold sweat broke out on his forehead. *Snap out of it,* he sternly ordered himself. *This is the twentieth century!*

It didn't help. So must those who had gone before have felt when they heard the cry of bloodhounds in pursuit and saw flickering lantern flames through the gloom of night. It took every ounce of courage Damon possessed to throw off the growing inertia that froze him in place. He clenched his hands until the nails cut into his sweaty palms. The pain freed him.

A moving van coasted to a stop. Damon subconsciously noted the absence of brake noise when it halted. Someone had done their work well. A raincoat-clad figure stepped from the passenger seat.

"Barton?"

Damon sagged with relief. He doubted anyone on earth possessed a voice like Agent Stone's. That the FBI man was personally on hand clearly indicated to what lengths the agent would go in order to stop Emil Schwartz and his cohorts. Damon stepped from the shadows.

"Here."

"All clear." A half-dozen figures in dark clothes sprang from the back of the moving van and silently slipped into the building. In an incredibly short time, they had the van loaded. Damon marveled at how quietly they worked. He saw shock in Nancy's eyes when they managed the few pieces of furniture so skillfully not even the closest neighbor was alarmed.

Neither of the Bartons looked back when the last item had been taken. Following Stone's terse commands, they slipped to the restored white Toyota. The agent had arranged for one of his officers to drive the red Honda. He had also made sure they had cell phones in the cars. "In case of changed instructions," he casually remarked.

Once inside the car, Nancy gave a little sob. Damon knew it stemmed from excitement and nerves strained to the breaking point. He laid his hand over hers and waited the eternity between the departure of the moving van and Stone's signal for them to follow.

Once on the street, he glanced back. The neighborhood slept, silent as a tomb. After a few moments a car lazily swung in behind them. Then another. A few blocks later, a third joined the procession.

"Agents?" Nancy whispered.

"Yes." At least he hoped so. It didn't seem possible anyone could penetrate the dragnet Stone had placed around them.

Mile by anxious mile they drove through the murky pre-dawn. Seattle dozed, as much as it ever did. Yet life went on beneath the uneasy truce created by night and fog. The nearly deserted streets didn't hide the fact that even now human termites might be plotting to undermine the basic freedoms America promised, and weaken her structure until it crumbled into a new world order.

Clockwork seemed crude and awkward compared with the carrying out of what Damon had facetiously dubbed Operation Move Bartons. The van stopped a few blocks from their newly-acquired home. So did Nancy and Damon. They waited until the red Toyota and two of the unmarked official cars passed them. Damon's thoughts went with Stone's team as they unlocked the house and checked it thoroughly. He dripped with sweat during the lifetime before the signal came for Nancy and him to proceed as planned. Her rapid breathing showed she experienced the same feelings.

When they reached the house and swung into the driveway, the neighborhood appeared as innocuous and safe as a locked church. Hope crept into Damon's heart and spread its wings. The move could not prevent further harassment at his and Dr. Cranston's office, but it might give them temporary security. In the meantime, Stone was stepping up his investigation.

Mrs. Buchanan had moved from the Bartons' house the day before, yet evidence of her caring remained. She had left the refrigerator stocked with milk, eggs, butter, and jam. A loaf of homemade bread tightly sealed in plastic wrap spelled welcome. So did the note that read,

Forgive a fanciful old lady, but I can't help feel-ing my house is as glad you are the ones to own and

*love it as I am. God care for you both. May you be
happy and blessed. I hope you will one day come
visit my family and me.*

Nancy had held up well through the whole ordeal. Now the
kindness and love in Mrs. Buchanan's farewell did what fear
had not been able to achieve. She buried her face in Damon's
jacket and let the tears come, but only for a moment.

"I—I can't cry now," she stammered. "Th—the van's
here."

He hugged her to him, reluctant to release her.

"I know. Stone wants everything moved in before daylight."

Nancy licked dry lips and managed a faint giggle.

"For the first time, I'm glad we don't own much furniture.
Right?"

"Right." He dropped a kiss on her upturned lips and sent a
measuring glance around the charming hall. "Most of it can
be stacked right here for now."

Not a wasted movement hampered the unloading of the
van. Obscured by the gray fog blanket, the move was completed soon.

"I feel like we should give you and your team moving
wages," Damon told Stone when they shook hands.

The FBI man's mouth set in a grim line. "We're after a lot
more than wages," he brusquely told the doctor and his wife.
A lightning glance surveyed the hall. "Nice place you have
here." His features softened into a smile. "A good night's
work. If we were followed, my name's not Stone." His face
immediately hardened again. "That doesn't mean you may not
be followed. Be careful. I'll try to keep that fool brother of
yours from doing anything stupid. Your guess is as good as
mine as to whether anyone can do that." He started out, then
sheepishly added, "Can't blame him too much. I'd feel the
same if you were my kid brother." He closed the front door

behind him with a little bang.

"So he's human after all!" Nancy exclaimed.

Damon felt a torrent of laughter coming. Her genuine surprise and amazed look unknotted his muscles. He clutched his stomach and roared. Nancy's mouth fell open, then she joined in. The first five minutes alone in their new home would forever remain in their minds as a time of cleansing laughter and tears.

"We'll have to make up a bed," Nancy reminded when they subsided. They mounted the staircase together hand-in-hand, man and wife against the world.

"Wrong, Mrs. Barton," Damon told her when they reached the master bedroom. He pointed. "Are those sheets, pillows, and cases brand new?"

Nancy fingered the delicately designed bed linen that invited weary bodies. Her eyes looked enormous. "Yes, except they aren't stiff. Damon, Mrs. Buchanan even washed them before making our bed. How kind!"

"If everyone who claims to be a Christian lived the way she does, what a different world it would be," Damon said soberly. On impulse he added, "Come back into the hall, will you?" He motioned toward the open bedroom door.

She blinked and obeyed, a wondering expression on her lovely face.

Damon put one arm beneath her knees, the other around her shoulders. "We're starting life in a new home. I want to carry you across the threshold."

Diamonds glittered in her lovely eyes. He strode inside, set Nancy down, and held her as if he would never let her go. His lips sought and found hers. For a time, all the Schwartzes and white supremacists in the world could not destroy their own little heaven on earth.

ↄ

Hours later, Nancy awakened to the first morning in her new home. Damon slept beside her. Memory of the night before swept through her. How impossible it all seemed—the secret, heavily-guarded trip through city streets. Reality surely must be the golden rays of sunlight reaching around the edge of the bedroom curtains to cast dancing reflections in a wall mirror.

Nancy turned on her side and looked at her husband. Exquisite pain pierced her. He looked so tired, thinner than she had ever seen him. God grant her strength, for Damon's sake even more than her own. The desire to be a true helpmate overwhelmed her. God had permitted her to become one with this prince among men. She must not fail him.

Damon stirred, then opened his eyes. Returning consciousness melted into the smile she cherished.

"Almost ten. Isn't it wonderful to have a few days off?" She started to sit up.

Damon held out a protesting hand. "Don't go. Let's pretend we're at a fine inn and room service will bring breakfast when we ring."

Nancy laughed. "The only room service at Barton Manor is me," she teased.

A poignant light crept into Damon's eyes. "Nancy, I hope God allows me to awaken with you beside me for at least another fifty years."

"Piker," she flouted through the rush of emotion his tender voice brought. "Why not go for seventy-five? Or a hundred?"

"That can't be properly answered with you so far away." He pulled her closer. Her head slipped naturally to the spot just above his steadily beating heart she had claimed for her own. Again the world and its problems receded, leaving only Nancy, her husband, and another precious memory engraved in her heart.

Their mood of deep joy continued during a far more leisurely breakfast than they usually enjoyed. Nancy had wisely packed the dishes, silver, toaster, and frying pan they would need the first day. After dedicating their new home to God, they returned the lemon yellow and spring green kitchen to its usual spotlessness. Next they unpacked, thrilling at how well their meager supply of furniture blended in with what they had bought from Mrs. Buchanan.

"We're like two children playing house," Damon observed.

Nancy held a pair of candlesticks her fellow nurses had given her as a wedding present. His words hit her like separate blows. One candlestick slipped from her nerveless hand. She wildly reached to catch it, but it fell to the hardwood floor. She gave a little moan.

"Are you all right?" Damon was instantly beside her. He picked up the candlestick. "Don't worry. It didn't break."

She shook her head. "I—it's not that."

He placed gentle hands on her shoulders and lightly shook her. "Nancy, what's wrong?"

"I've been so happy. How could I forget?"

"Darling, it is right for us to forget." He held her close. "Even if our enemies find us again, this is our time to rejoice and be glad, to appreciate the simple joy of being together." He looked deep into her eyes. "Would you rather have gone somewhere away from Seattle? It's not too late."

"No. I'd rather be here in our own home with you than anywhere else in the whole world. It's perfect." *It would be even more perfect if we knew someday Jason Street could be here with us,* her heart reminded. Words trembled on Nancy's lips, a plea to save Jason. She stilled them, but with a pang. To speak meant shattering the fragile peace they shared.

Nancy wrapped her arms around her husband and whispered, "You're right, my darling. Today is ours." Yet some of the brightness in her heart dimmed, as if a cloud had come between the sun and Seattle, obscuring its bright splendor. It took all of Nancy's dramatic ability to retrieve the specialness she knew both she and Damon needed to arm themselves for whatever lay ahead.

❧

Several miles away, Curtis Barton paced the floor of a motel room, obscure because it could be any of a thousand rooms in any city. His mind cried out for action. Instead, he flipped on the TV and dropped heavily to a bed that cloned countless other motel beds. Used to taking life by the horns, the stress of waiting sawed on his nerves. Back and forth. Back and forth. Stone's furtive call the night before telling him all went as planned had alleviated some of his worry, but Curtis chafed under the restriction of having nothing to do but wait.

Why hadn't he thought to grab a paperback from the rack by the chain restaurant where he ate breakfast? Maybe it would take his mind off the mess he'd unwittingly created. Stretching out and folding his arms behind him, Curtis stared at the jabbering TV. His lip curled. Daytime programming would drive a person insane if he had to watch much of it.

He punched the remote control. Blessed silence filled the room. He looked at his watch. Had it stopped? No. When he held it to his ear, the faithful ticking beat like a hammer in his brain. In desperation, Curtis scanned the room. He read straight through a TV listing sheet, and groaned. Too bad they didn't let him program the channels. He'd air something more than tripe.

He crumpled the listing into a ball and threw it across the room. It landed on a Gideon Bible that lay next to the TV, like an accusing finger pointing out his shortcomings. His face twisted and he stared at the ceiling.

"Can't get away from it, can I?" he muttered. "Ever since I saw the trapper fall. It could have been me. Would have been, if he hadn't shoved me back and took my place. What made him do it?"

The mystery haunted him. He mentally replayed the horrifying scene in Idaho again and again, searching for reasons and coming up emptyhanded. In all their time together, the trapper hadn't talked about God. Yet something inherently decent in the man had sent him to his death to save Curtis Barton's skin.

Memories of himself and Damon at their mama's knee

attacked Curtis like battering rams. Too bad he and his brother couldn't go back to those days and start all over. Would it do any good? If he had a second chance, would he heed Mama's teachings about Jesus, God's Son who came to save the world?

"God, even if You're real like Damon and Nancy and Mama said, You wouldn't have anything to do with me." Cold in spite of the warm room, he turned on his side and curled into a ball. A harsh laugh rang out. For the first time in his life, Curtis Barton felt the weight and depth of his sins.

"It's too late for me, but it isn't fair for Damon to have to pay for what I've done."

It wasn't fair for the trapper, either. Or Jesus.

Curtis' heart leapt to his throat. He sprang from the bed. Who had spoken? He glanced at the bolted door, intact against intruders. Cautiously peeping around the window blind, he saw no movement to indicate a presence. The feeling someone or something had defied the laws of nature and entered his motel room swelled and grew. He felt a film of sweat cover his face and sank back to the bed. Was he going crazy?

The feeling persisted and strengthened, until he cried out, "Who is it?"

Only silence answered.

Curtis Barton had prided himself on fearlessness for years. He had fought against those who crossed him. Yet never had he experienced the stark terror that now engulfed him, or felt that unseen forces threatened to rend him limb from limb. How could a man fight what he could not see?

His roving gaze fell on the Bible. *Holy Bible, King James Version*, the cover proclaimed. He reached it in a single bound and clutched it to his chest like a shield. Stories of those who overcame evil swam through his brain. Could the Book in his hands free him from this waking nightmare? He frantically opened it, turning pages so rapidly some tore. Nothing he read rid him of the ever-increasing horror, the knowledge his sanity, perhaps his life, hung in the balance.

"God, help me!"

It came out as a whisper. He turned more pages. Someone before him had highlighted Luke 5:32:

> *And Jesus answering said unto them, They that are*
> *whole need not a physician; but they that are sick.*

A great sob rose from the depths of the suffering man's soul. Whole? When had he ever been whole? He had been only part of a person from the time as a young boy when he weakly allowed his brother to bear the blame for his actions! Sick. That was it. Sick of heart, mind, and soul, in need of healing.

The knuckles of Curtis' hands showed white where he clutched the Bible. He read the final words of the Scripture.

> *I came not to call the righteous, but sinners to*
> *repentance.*

In the history of the world, had there ever been a greater sinner than Curtis Barton? Shame threatened to consume him. He kept one finger in the Bible for fear he would lose the place and fearfully turned more pages. Anxiety mounted. He found nothing that helped until he came to John 3:16, also highlighted. He could almost hear his mother's voice, as she quoted it again and again. *For God so loved the world, that He gave His only begotten Son, that whosoever believeth in Him, should not perish, but have everlasting life.*

Curtis read on.

> *For God sent not His Son into the world to con-*
> *demn the world; but that the world through Him*
> *might be saved.*

The Bible fell to the coverlet. Curtis slipped to his knees

beside the bed. Did 'whoever' and 'the world' include him?

In the quiet broken only by his own heavy breathing, he fancied he heard the words: *For God so loved Curtis. . .* A cry he had heard a hundred times as a child, the plea of those seeking freedom from sin, burst out. "God, I believe! Have mercy on me, a sinner." After a long time he added, "Because of Your Son." Tears he thought had long since dried up forever fell in sheets. They dampened the hands pressed over his eyes, the woven bedspread beneath his hot face.

Peace came slowly. First, a gentle calm he did not know existed in a violent world. It spread like dandelion fluff scattered by the wind. Every part of Curtis's body came alive and tingled with unexplainable joy. He lay back down on the bed, holding the Bible with reverent fingers. After a time, he quietly turned the pages once more, thanking God for those who had placed it in the room, for the hand that had highlighted the verses. He stopped at John 14:27.

Peace I leave with you, my peace I give unto you; not as the world giveth, give I unto you. Let not your heart be troubled, neither let it be afraid.

The last of his shackles snapped and fell away. Even the blurred image of his face in the mirror across the room did not look the same.

"Thank You, Lord," Curtis brokenly whispered.

He threw wide the window curtain and let the light shine on him with full force. Yet the hot sun was as nothing compared with the Son-light that had touched Curtis Barton—and changed him forever.

twelve

For three idyllic days, Dr. and Mrs. Nancy Barton spent a second honeymoon in their new home. They left only once, to stock up on groceries at the closest supermarket. What joy to arrange the spacious rooms to their heart's content, to work in the yard and repeatedly give thanks for the peaceful, tree-lined streets and balmy, flower-scented air.

The neighbors on both sides appeared friendly. A slight look of surprise showed in a heavy-set man's eyes when he saw the Bartons in their yard. It faded so rapidly Nancy couldn't be sure it had really been there. The man came to the low fence and grinned.

"I see we have a doctor in the neighborhood." He nodded toward the discreet caduceus and Shepherd of Love hospital sticker in the lower left corner of their windshield. "My name's Simmons."

"Damon Barton." He laughed and waved at a disreputable Nancy covered with dirt from working in the rich earth. "My wife's a nurse, although right now, she looks more like a professional gardener."

"Mrs. Buchanan sure kept her place up," the neighbor commented, with a satisfied glance at the yard. "All the folks around here do." After a few more pleasantries, he excused himself and disappeared into the house.

"Am I being overly suspicious, or did I detect a note of doubt that we'd maintain the property according to neighborhood standards?" Nancy demanded in a low voice.

Damon sighed.

"We have to expect it, I suppose. It comes with being the first African Americans on the block. Actually, it would probably be the same for anyone new to this particular area. It's so well-kept no one would want a family to move in and let their place go."

"They won't have reason to complain about us," Nancy told him, even though the thought of being on trial hurt. She dug furiously at a lone dandelion that had the temerity to poke its golden head up through the green-velvet lawn. "At least it appears there's no—what did you call it? Gentleman's agreement?"

"Thank God for that," Damon fervently told her. He smiled. "You don't convince others you're an asset to a community by coming on like Superman. We're simply going to be ourselves and give people time to know us."

"Right." She tossed the dandelion into a yard debris container and brushed dirt from her gloved hands. "They won't be able to resist us, once they learn how nice we are. Especially since you're a doctor," she teased and dropped her voice to a bass rumble. "Ahem, Dr. Barton, I know you aren't on duty, but I have this pain and I was just wondering. . ."

The laughter that followed washed away the tiny feeling of depression their new neighbor had left in Nancy's heart like the sting of an unsuspected nettle.

◆

It took all the caring nurse's willpower to keep from interrupting her days off the job by calling Pediatrics to check on Jason. A dozen times she reached for the phone and withdrew her slim, dark hand. *Better to leave well enough alone.* If she discovered the little boy was unhappy, it would spoil things for both her and Damon.

"Besides," she told her reflection while brushing her hair at bed time on the third night, "I don't have the right to allow Jason to grow any more attached than he already is. It isn't fair to him. Or to me."

The hairbrush stopped its rhythmic stroking. Her eyes misted. If only she could open her arms and home to the orphaned child! A tiny ember of hope glowed in her heart. There had been no unusual incidents since they came to the new house. If things continued as they were, perhaps she could broach the subject to Damon soon.

Any spark of approaching her husband died to ashes overnight. An early morning telephone call from an unidentified person advised them to come outside as soon as possible. Tossing robes over their pajamas, Damon and Nancy raced downstairs and out into a glorious summer morning. Nothing appeared unusual, until they looked at the garage door. Ugly black swastikas marred its surface, along with a too-familiar slogan: *DIE, NIGGERS.*

A small crowd of neighbors had already assembled. Nancy heard their whispers even through her shock.

"Who did it?"

"Why?"

"Terrible!"

"We've never had this kind of thing here before."

Mr. Simmons pushed through the crowd.

"What's going on out here?" He stared, turned brick red, and clenched his hands into fists. "This is inexcusable! You there, Adams," he bellowed. "Call the police. Bring paint and brushes from my garage. Dr. and Mrs. Barton, go back in the house. We'll take care of this."

Adams hurried to obey the commanding voice. Nancy felt like crying at burly Mr. Simmons' rush to their defense. She turned toward the front door but paused when Damon ordered, "Thanks, but don't touch anything until the police come."

Minutes or hours later, Nancy never knew which, three Seattle police cars arrived. Hands on hips, the officers surveyed the defacement.

"Dr. Barton, I have to level with you," the clear-eyed captain said. "We'll do what we can, but there's not much chance we'll learn who did this. Did anyone see or hear anything out of the ordinary?" he asked the crowd.

Unless someone present possessed greater acting ability than current Hollywood idols, those gathered knew nothing about the incident.

When the squad cars drove away, Damon told Simmons and Adams, who had returned with bucket and brushes, "Leave it for now, will you? I have a reason," he added when they gave him a startled glance.

"Whatever you say." Disapproval oozed from the Good Samaritan neighbors. The crowd slowly dispersed, with many backward glances and much murmuring.

"Stone needs to be told," Damon explained when he and Nancy got back inside. "You also need to go to work. I'll call and arrange with Dr. Cranston to cover my morning appointments, then drive you to Shepherd of Love."

"All right. What about breakfast?" Her stomach revolted at the thought.

Damon grimaced. "We need to eat. Tea and toast will probably stay down the best." He took Nancy's hand. "Darling, it's ugly, but something good has already come out of it. Simmons, Adams and the others are backing us."

"I know." She drew in a quivering, painful breath. "It's the only good thing I can see. Damon, it isn't just us. We have dedicated our home and our lives to God. Whoever is persecuting us is also waging war against our Master."

"He will defend us," Damon quietly promised.

"I know."

Nancy did know, but her heart felt like a chunk of lead lying heavy and stiff in her chest. It took a real effort to smile when Damon kissed her good-bye at the staff entrance to Shepherd of Love.

"Stay with Patti and Shina until I come for you," he told her.

It seemed years instead of a few weeks since Damon had told her the same thing after the trashing of his and Dr. Cranston's office. Nancy promised, went into the building, and walked to Pediatrics with slow steps. It didn't help her depression when she saw Jason hop from his bed and race down the ward, Susan Devers in swift pursuit.

He flung his arms around Nancy and cried, "Why did you leave me?"

If Nancy had not been a trained and experienced nurse, she would have followed her inclination to sit down on the floor and howl along with him. Instead, she dropped to one knee and patted Jason's tousled head.

"My goodness! Is all that noise coming out of one little boy? I'm sure Nurse Susan told you I had a few days off work."

"Y—yes." Sobs dwindled to sniffles.

"You knew I'd come back, didn't you?"

"I was a—afraid. Th—there was a s—siren." He burrowed his wet face in the tunic of the yellow pants suit she automatically reached for when she felt the lowest.

"There'th nothing to be 'fraid of," the small girl in the closest bed lisped through the space left by two missing front teeth. Her blue eyes looked enormous under a king-sized bandage. "That'th an amb'lanth. It bringth people who are thick and hurt. The doctorth and nurtheth help God fix 'em. Mommy thaid tho, and Mommy's alwath right."

"Head wound suffered when she fell from a swing," Susan filled in, voice low. "It knocked her out for a time, so we kept her overnight. Her name's Justine." The LPN chuckled and her eyes twinkled. "The fall thertainly, I mean certainly, didn't hurt her speech. Justine's been talking nonstop ever since she regained consciousness."

The child smiled enchantingly and stuck her pink tongue in the front gap. "Did you come in an amb'lanth?" she asked Jason.

He cringed and shook his head. Nancy felt a tremor go through him.

"Dr. Barton brought Jason. And Nurse Nancy Barton is

going to wash his face and hands so he will be ready for breakfast."

She caught Jason up in her arms and marched down the ward.

She couldn't outmaneuver the irrepressible Justine.

"I like you, Jathon," she called after them.

"Looks like you have a new friend," Nancy teased. She quickly settled him and bathed his flushed face.

He solemnly wagged his head from side to side. The unhappiness in his eyes smote her like the flat edge of a sword when he whispered, "No. She will go away and leave me. Everyone goes away."

Nancy knew how important it was that he not allow that thought to become a fixation.

"People come back, Jason. I did. Dr. Barton will."

He turned his face toward the window and stared out. Nancy's gaze followed his. She had the feeling Jason wasn't seeing the sunshine, green grass, or the multitude of birds and blooming flowers.

He tilted his head back and asked, "Is heaven back of the sky?"

Nancy never patronized children by giving them false information. "No one knows for sure exactly where heaven is," she explained. "I like to think it is just where you said: back of the sky. We do know heaven is such a wonderful place Jesus said none of us can even imagine its beauty! Think of that."

Jason fell silent for a long while. Nancy wondered what went on in the mind she had discovered was both keen and intelligent. He kept his eyes turned toward the spreading patch of blue sky frosted with marshmallow clouds until the breakfast trays arrived, then forlornly asked, "Do Mama and Daddy and the others get oatmeal for breakfast? We always had it when they were here."

The image of a family gathered around a breakfast table danced before Nancy. She pictured their faces, happy in spite of their humble surroundings and few worldly goods. Then, arson. Flames and smoke. Screams and death. Nancy bit her lip to stem the rising tide of nausea. The carnage had not ended with the Street family. A second house and a third in the same general area had been torched since Jason came to Shepherd of Love. The police had two men in custody. Nancy rejoiced, hoping they were the guilty parties. It would mean an end to the rampage that resulted in tragedy for the living, as well as the dead.

How long, Lord? her tender heart cried. *How long must Your children pay for the crimes of others?*

Jason tugged at her sleeve.

She forced a laugh and said "I don't know about oatmeal in heaven, but yours is getting cold. Down the hatch, Mister Street." Her attempt at gaiety won a half-smile and a spirited attack on the bowl of cereal. Nancy thought of her own sketchy tea and toast breakfast. Lunch couldn't come any too soon for her today.

One good thing about Pediatrics was the demands of patients left little time for woolgathering. The most troubled nurses soon learned to park their problems outside the door and give full attention to the needs inside. So did Nancy.

Patti Thompson and Shina Ito hailed her with delight when she reached the cool green staff dining room.

"How's the lady of leisure?" the pretty blonde demanded. "Three whole days off all together sounds heavenly to me." She stretched her lithe, blue-uniformed body. "Out-patient this morning was the original madhouse." Patti rushed into a description of frustrated patients, a doctor held up by traffic, and the ensuing traffic jam in the department she loved.

Shina gave Nancy a quiet smile, but didn't tease Patti as usual. The Pediatrics nurse felt her friend's dark eyes saw far more than the equally caring but less observant Patti. Nancy wondered how Shina's star-crossed love affair was progressing. The maze of moving and Curtis's return had left no time for sharing confidences. Nancy's suspicions proved well-founded when the tiny pink-clad nurse linked arms with her and they walked back to their duty stations after lunch.

"Are you really, truly all right?" Shina asked.

Memory of the ugly swastikas on the garage door caused Nancy to wordlessly shake her head.

"Meet me after work?" Shina pleaded. Her hand tightened on Nancy's arm.

Nancy nodded.

"I'm praying for you," the smaller nurse reminded.

Nancy's voice returned. "I know. Prayers are all that are getting me through."

She left a concerned Shina outside the Obstetrics door and hurried to her ward.

Somehow she made it through the rest of the day. Unable to concentrate on reports, she spent time with each individual child in her charge, to their unbounded delight. Their trusting faces, their faith in the doctors' and nurses' ability to take care of everything from Jimmy's owie to Tara's broken ankle brought a certain comfort. For the millionth time, she thanked God for being permitted to help His children, and passionately wished she could do even more.

On break with Susan in the middle of the afternoon shift, she relaxed and described the home she and Damon had acquired.

"I can't wait to see it," her friend exclaimed.

Happiness fled like chalk dust beneath a wet sponge. "It may be awhile."

"Do you want to talk about it?" The LPN bluntly asked.

Nancy shrugged. "Why not? The evening news may report it. We awoke to more harassment, if you can call swastikas and another racially related death threat at our new place harassment." She couldn't bring herself to repeat the obscenity spray-painted on the garage door.

Susan's face pinched. Her capable hand covered Nancy's dark one.

"This can't be random," she slowly said.

"It isn't." Nancy clung to Susan's fingers until the older nurse winced. "I can't tell you what's back of it." Her shoulders slumped. "We thought moving might help the situation." Her eyes burned and she stared at Susan. "Everything's so confusing. The neighbors rallied and planned to repaint. They were furious. There's never been a similar incident in the area." Discouragement touched her voice. "I wonder if Damon and I even have the right to stay. What if we bring danger to the neighborhood we chose because of its peace and security?"

Susan had no answer, but the firm pressure of her strong hand silently offered the only comfort she could give.

A short time later, Nancy posed the same question to a wide-eyed Shina. The little nurse sat on her sofa and poured tea into porcelain cups. She looked more doll-like than ever in her favorite Japanese kimono.

"Do we have the right?" Nancy asked her. "Does anyone have the right to put others in danger?"

Shina shook her head. "I don't know, Nancy. I do understand how you feel. On the other hand, the persecution isn't about an African-American couple moving into the neighborhood, is it? The same thing happened before you found and purchased Mrs. Buchanan's house." She handed Nancy a steaming cup of fragrant orange spice tea, delicately flavored with wild honey.

Nancy found it hard to swallow the tempting brew. She set her cup down and confessed, "Shina, I am about at the end of my rope. I know God loves Damon and me. I know He is mindful of us." She stared at the other girl, eyes gritty with fatigue and hopelessness. "It's just that now when I need Him the most, He seems so far away I can't reach Him."

Shina's eyes widened. A peculiar expression came to her face. For a full minute she returned Nancy's stare, then rose from the sofa in one fluid motion. Determination etched itself into her face.

"I'll be right back," she mumbled. She headed for the bedroom, leaving an open-mouthed Nancy asking herself what possessed her friend. The click of a typewriter followed.

Nancy couldn't believe her ears. What on earth! Shina returned immediately, a sheet of paper in one hand. She unsmilingly seated herself. Nancy wondered at the almost fearful expression in Shina's face, and the tense way she clutched the paper. Shina's eyes pleaded. *For what? Understanding? Why?*

"What is it?" Nancy gently asked, her own concerns dissipating before the cry for help in Shina's eyes.

She replied in a voice so low Nancy had to lean forward to catch the words. "This is hard. I'm glad Patti had a date with Charles. I don't know if I could do this if she were here, and I must." She sent a beseeching look Nancy's way.

"Do what, Shina?"

Words tumbled out. "It never happened to me before. It hasn't since." With a visible effort, Shina steadied her voice. "Remember the night Dr. Barton was so late and you came home with me?"

Nancy thought of the day the Barton/Cranston office had been trashed. That night she and Damon first met Stone, and she had identified the sketch of Emil Schwartz as the man at Anthony's Homeport.

"Only too well." She added, "You told me about Kevin and your parents."

"Yes." Shina twisted her hands in obvious agitation. "After you and Damon went to the police station, I prayed." Shame filled her dark eyes. "For myself and Kevin, until I realized how selfish that was when you were facing persecution. Anyway, I knelt and poured out everything I could think of. After a time peace came." She paused. "I took out my journal and wrote in it for the first time in months. My pen raced over the pages. Nancy, nothing I wrote was about Kevin or me. Every word concerned your and Damon's needs."

Nancy's hand flew to her throat. She braced herself, because the look in Shina's face said she had not finished the story.

Shina's body went rigid. Her voice dropped to a whisper. Her eyes grew enormous.

"The last few lines startled me," she said. "I didn't understand why I had written them. I felt frightened and unsure of myself. I studied my Bible for a long time. I also asked God whether I should tell you what happened."

Nancy's nerves screamed. "What happened?"

Shina's lips trembled. "I fell asleep. I awoke feeling if or when God wanted me to share, I'd know. And that you would be able to discern if it was my concern—or of God. I believe now is the time." She handed Nancy the paper.

Nancy's blurred gaze rested on the single, typed paragraph.

> *Nancy and Damon shall be tried, but not more than they will be able to stand. God will never forsake them. One day, the glowing embers of hatred that spawns persecution will be stamped out of their lives. They will see how God's hand guided and cared for them during their most fiery trials.*

Nancy's hands tightened convulsively on the paper. She read the words again, feeling them brand themselves into her soul. Was that the sound of the snapping of invisible chains that had bound her?

"Thank God!" she breathed. Tears spilled. She opened her arms and embraced Shina. The page fell between them—the page containing the message a wise and all-loving heavenly Father in heaven had prepared, for the exact time Nancy and Damon most needed it.

thirteen

After Damon delivered Nancy to work, he hurried home. FBI Agent Stone stood in the driveway examining the graffiti on the Bartons' garage door. His countenance matched his name.

"MOS," he spit out.

"MOS?" Damon asked.

"More of the same." Stone stared at the ugly, threatening words. "I'll stake my job on this being part of a pattern of escalating harassment." He squared his shoulders. "In a way I'm glad."

"What!" The doctor's exclamation cracked like an over-heated test tube.

Stone's mouth twitched into the grimmest travesty of a smile Damon had ever seen.

"I'm no Pollyanna, but things could be a whole lot worse. What if you were being harassed by more than one party or parties?"

Damon chilled at the menace in the agent's voice.

"Thanks a lot. That's exactly what I need to hear right now," he said sarcastically.

"Look, Dr. Barton, this way we can keep our focus narrow instead of having to broaden it and include other factors."

"I know. Sorry."

"Don't be." Stone's gaze bore into Damon with the agent's usual shiny, drill-like expression. "Anyone who's putting up with what you and your wife are just now has the right to spout off now and then. Just don't let it affect—" He broke off when the telephone shrilled inside the house. "I thought I told you to get an unlisted number."

The phone screeched again. Damon licked his lips. "We did."

"Who has the number?"

"Nancy. The hospital. Dr. Cranston." Damon paused. Dread surged through him. "Curtis."

Stone swore. "If that fool is calling you, so help me, I'll break his neck and enjoy doing it." He followed Damon's long strides to the front door, waited until Damon unlocked it, then unceremoniously brushed him aside.

"Let me answer, just in case." He grabbed the phone.

In case what? Damon dully had time to wonder before Stone barked. "Yeah?"

Damon froze. Evidently the caller asked if this were the Barton residence because the agent snapped, "Who wants to know?" He paused a moment and his tone of voice changed. "Yeah, I'll take it." He covered the mouthpiece and whispered, "Western Union."

"Western Union?" A galaxy of thoughts whirled through Damon's brain. Western Union wouldn't have the unlisted number. Those persons who did would call, not use a messenger service.

Stone yanked a stubby pencil and a crumpled piece of paper from a pocket. "Shoot," he told the operator.

Did he have to choose that particular word, Damon sickly wondered. He held his breath while Stone scribbled, ordered, "Repeat," and cradled the phone. He looked puzzled. "Might be an address, except it has too many numbers. I also never heard of a Luke Street or Avenue."

"Luke Street! Is that what the telegram said?" Damon demanded.

"Not street. Just Luke 15171824." Stone peered at the scrawled paper and handed it to Damon. "What about St. Luke's, as in a church, or hospital?"

St. Luke. Damon stared at the cryptic message. Somewhere in the dim recesses of his mind a bell rang, a tiny light flared. He closed his eyes and concentrated. Luke 15171824. The persistent bell and light increased, sending blood pumping through his body in a rushing stream. "Maybe it's not a place."

"Then what—?"

Damon ignored him, hurried to a nearby bookcase and snatched out a Bible. The feeling of being on the right track grew like sunflowers in August. He turned pages.

"Here it is. The book of Luke. The first one might be chapter one. That would make the five and the second one a verse number." He read verse 51 aloud: "He hath shewed strength with his arm; he hath scattered the proud in the imagination of their hearts." Damon looked at Stone. "It makes sense after this morning."

Stone looked skeptical. "Your enemies, actually your brother's enemies, will eventually get your unlisted number. They have spies everywhere. It's highly unlikely they could get it this fast. Besides, what chance is there of (1) their knowing exactly where to look in the Bible, and (2) knowing you'd be able to decode their message? Slime isn't noted for being subtle."

"Right. Besides, Luke doesn't have 71 chapters and chapter seven, verse one is totally irrelevant."

Stone held out his hand for the paper. "Hmm. Luke 15171824. Maybe it's chapter 15, not chapter one. Check it out, will you?"

Damon turned to Luke 15:1. "Nothing here."

He flipped the page and gave a sharp exclamation. He could feel a tiny pulse pounding in his temple. Hope that had surged and lain dormant for years threatened to choke him.

"Listen to this, Stone. Luke 15:17 says, 'And when he came to himself, he said, How many hired servants of my father's have bread enough and to spare, and I perish with hunger.' " His voice quickened. "Verse 18 and 24 tell the rest of the story, 'I will arise and go to my father, and will say unto him, Father, I have sinned against heaven, and before thee. For this my son was dead and is alive again; he was lost, and is found. . .' " The Bible fell from his unsteady hands.

"So? I don't get it."

Even the rasp of Stone's hand across his chin couldn't annoy Damon.

"Curtis has found the Lord."

The agent looked at Damon as if the doctor had suddenly taken leave of his senses.

"Excuse me?"

Tenuous belief turned to knowledge. Damon proudly threw his head back. "My brother knew I would eventually decipher the message and recognize the story. He's joked about being the Prodigal Son more times than I can count."

Stone's jaw sagged. He looked disappointed. "So all this means is that your brother got religion?" He looked more sour than ever. "I thought it might be something important to the case."

"Not religion," Damon softly corrected. "Faith, repentance, and acceptance of the Lord Jesus Christ. It may not help solve the case, but it's the most important thing that could ever happen to Curtis or anyone."

"Whatever." The agent brushed the little sermon aside. "Now, here's what we're going to do." He rapidly outlined the next few steps of the plan his fertile brain had formulated in the last few minutes.

Damon nodded at appropriate places, glad for the ability to hear and assimilate while his heart sang. *Curtis saved. After all these years of praying, Curtis has accepted Christ! How? When? Where? Why at this particular moment?* He burned to know details, even while rejoicing in the simple fact his brother was no longer lost, but found.

At last Stone left. Damon glanced at his watch and reached for the phone to call Nancy. He slowly let his hand fall away. This news was too precious to be sandwiched between Nancy's nursing duties. Tonight they would savor it together, like the fragrance from a scented candle.

Unwilling to leave the mutilated garage door as a symbol of violence in the peaceful neighborhood, Damon called his office and reported the new trouble to Dr. Cranston. His partner immediately ordered Damon to take the rest of the day off and get the mess cleaned up. Simmons, Adams, and the other neighbors had long since left for work, leaving the painting supplies behind. Damon scrubbed, sanded, primed and waited for the primer to dry. He also found paint in the garage neatly marked *Garage Door.* How orderly Mrs. Buchanan had been! The doctor sobered. She would feel terrible to know what had befallen her neighborhood and the couple who purchased her long-term home.

"God," he prayed. "Please help stop this hatred."

The simple prayer, the brilliant, paint-drying day, and delight over the telegram message lifted Damon's spirits. While applying a top coat of paint with smooth, sure strokes of the paint pad, he burst into song.

"Praise God, from whom all blessings flow; Praise Him, all creatures here below; Praise Him above, ye heav'nly host; Praise Father, Son, and Holy Ghost. A-men."

Before the last, resonant note of the amen died, an amazed voice demanded, "Hey, Doc, what kind of man are you, anyway?"

Damon turned. Simmons stood just behind him, a bewildered look on his genial face. "I never heard of a man who sang praises for a death threat!"

Laughter bubbled up in Damon and erupted like a geyser. "I haven't, either. Believe me, I'm not thanking God for what happened this morning."

"Then how come. . ." Simmons' questioning voice trailed off.

Damon started to share the wonderful news about Curtis, but bit his tongue. He couldn't explain without going into a lot more details than Stone wanted disclosed at this time.

"Do you have time to hear a story?"

"Sure." Simmons grinned and folded his arms over his stocky chest. "Came home early to see if I could help here, but I see you've about got it licked."

"Right." Damon gave another expert swipe with the paint pad.

"So are you going to tell your story or not?"

"Sure." Damon parked the paint pad on the tray and stretched. "When I was in college, I used to ride the same bus every morning. I got to know the driver and most of his morning passengers. What a great guy that driver was! Always had a smile for everyone." Regret filled him. "I need to look him up some time." Damon shook himself out of his reverie.

"Anyway, one of the morning regulars was a grouch." Damon rolled his eyes and groaned. "Stacked up alongside of Scrooge, that guy would make old Ebenezer look like the world's softest pussycat. Every day when the driver smiled and said good morning, Grouch First Class sneered and said, 'What's good about it?' before marching to his seat.

"I finally got so disgusted I asked the driver, 'Why bother with the jerk? You know when you wish him good morning all he will do is gripe.' I'll never forget what the bus driver said."

Simmons shuffled his feet impatiently. "Well?"

"He looked straight into my eyes, every trace of humor gone. Then he quietly told me, 'Son, I refuse to let anyone decide what kind of day or life I'm going to have, except me and God.' "

"Heavy!" A reluctant smile crept over Simmons' alert face. "Makes sense, though." He started toward his house next door. "Since you don't need me, guess I'll crank up the old lawn mower." He paused. "You kinda remind me of Mrs. Buchanan. She used to say stuff like that."

An impish desire to tease made Damon say, "Then I can't be all bad, can I?"

"Naw." Simmons turned red at the blunt response, but a glint of mischief creased the skin at the corner of his eyes and mouth.

"No one who's like Mrs. Buchanan could ever be all bad." Guffawing at his own wit, Simmons grinned again and headed for home.

Damon not only had the garage door glistening in its new coat of paint by the time to go get Nancy, it had dried enough for him to close and lock. He'd take no chances on unwelcome visitors, even with Simmons mowing and highly visible.

"I hope she had a good day," he reflected on the short drive. Nancy's brief call to let him know she'd be with Shina when he came had given little indication. He suspected others had been around when she called. Love for him rang in her voice, but she sounded more reserved than when calling in privacy.

Nancy must have been watching the parking lot from the window of Shina's apartment. Before he could stop the motor and get out, she flew to him. Damon could scarcely believe his eyes. Where was the troubled, discouraged nurse he had delivered to Shepherd of Love just a few hours earlier? This radiant woman in her jonquil yellow uniform little resembled that woebegone creature. Dark eyes sparkled. Even white teeth flashed in a real smile, not the half-hearted attempt Damon knew had been the best she could manage for him earlier.

Nancy didn't wait for him to open the door. She piled into the bucket seat, waved a sheet of white paper, and announced, "Damon, God is so good!"

He thought of the enigmatic telegram message that had baffled Stone.

"Yes, He is," Damon fervently agreed. "What's that you're holding?" He reached for the fluttering page. "Whatever it is has certainly made a difference in you."

Nancy moved the page out of reach.

"You'll understand when I explain," she breathlessly promised. Leaning over to kiss him, she whispered, "Oh, Damon, how can we ever doubt Him?" She didn't wait for an answer but sat up and buckled her seat belt. "Maybe we should wait until we get home."

"It isn't far," he reminded. "I repainted."

"Good." A shadow crossed Nancy's finely sculpted features but another warm smile chased it away as March winds drive rain from the horizon.

Her excitement and anticipation magnified his own.

"I also have wonderful news, which we'll keep until we get home," he told her.

Never had the short distance seemed so far, yet in a short while they turned into the driveway of their recently acquired home. The freshly painted garage door bore no trace it had ever been anything other than in its present spotless state. Damon pushed the opener, drove in, and closed it behind them.

"All right, Nancy, talk before you explode," Damon teased when they got in the house.

It only took a few sentences for Nancy to explain Shina's concern and what followed that recent night that now seemed a lifetime ago.

"She wasn't sure whether she should ever tell us," Nancy whispered. "The next morning she felt strongly that if or when God wanted us to know, she'd be aware of it. Today she felt the time had come." The fingers that held out the paper trembled.

Wondering, Damon took it. He focused on the single, typed paragraph.

Nancy and Damon shall be tried, but not more than they will be able to stand. God will never forsake them. One day, the glowing embers of hatred

*that spawns persecution will be stamped out of their
lives. They will see how God's hand guided and
cared for them during their most fiery trials.*

A tremor went through Damon. He looked from the page to
Nancy, restored from a despairing lady to the strong and
courageous woman he loved and secretly depended on, far
more than she realized.

"Nancy?" Emotion robbed him of further speech and he
had to wait for a moment and allow it to recede. "Some of
this has already come to pass."

Her eyes widened. "What do you mean?"

"I received a telegram from Curtis today."

Shock sprang to Nancy's eyes. Damon saw her throat con-
vulse for a moment.

"There's nothing to fear," he told her. "Far from it. I don't
know how or where. I don't know why at this time, but the
message can only mean one thing: Curtis has accepted Christ
into his heart and life!" Damon caught up the still-open Bible
from the table where he had dropped it when he realized the
full portent of the telegram. In broken tones he read Luke 15,
verses 17, 18, and 24.

Nancy flew into her husband's arms like a homing pigeon.

"You're right," she cried. "This makes everything worth
it." She hugged him, laughing and weeping at the same time.
"We need to celebrate. If only we could tell Curtis how happy
we are!" Some of her happiness dimmed. "We can't, can we?
Agent Stone won't tell us where he is, will he?" When
Damon shook his head, she added, "Then we'll thank God
and trust that Curtis already knows."

She dropped to her knees. Damon knelt beside her. In
heartfelt gratitude, they thanked God for His promises. They
also thanked Him for the greater miracle, the entrance of
Christ into a sinful heart made clean through the matchless
gift of God's only Son.

Even the prayers didn't fully satisfy the Bartons' longing to praise their Master. "Suppose there's a church nearby that's having a service tonight?" Damon wondered aloud. "Let's make a quick dinner and go on an exploring tour. So far we haven't had time to familiarize ourselves with all the area."

"Sounds great." Nancy gracefully rose and extended a helping hand to her husband. She squeezed his and her eyes danced.

"We can save time if a certain handsome doctor doesn't mind setting out leftovers while I shower and change."

"Do I get a tip?" He smirked at her and pulled her close.

"Mercenary, aren't you? Not that I mind." She stood on tiptoe and kissed him.

Damon's hold tightened. The touch of her soft lips sent another prayer of thankfulness up from his overflowing heart. More tribulation surely lay before them, as for anyone dedicated to serving the Lord. Yet with Nancy beside him, God's assurance with them, and Curtis finding the long and tortuous way home, surely they would make it through.

❧

Earlier that afternoon, Shina Ito watched from her apartment window while Nancy flew to Damon. A mist of unshed tears softened Shina's velvety eyes. Her heart ached. Would the day come when she'd have the right to fly to her beloved? To seek love, comfort, and protection in Kevin Hyde's arms?

Shina turned from the window and sadly shook her head. Her father showed no signs of abandoning his firm position that his only daughter must marry someone of her own race. Worse, he had forbade her to mention it. Arms folded, face impassive, he told her, "I have promised to think on this. Until then, you must remain silent, my daughter."

Rebellion against old ways and tradition rose within her. Only the Fifth Commandment kept her from protesting. Now she repeated it. " 'Honor thy father and thy mother: that thy days may be long upon the land which the Lord thy God giveth thee.' " (Exodus 20:12, KJV)

Shina bowed her head. Could she disobey her father, even for Kevin? Sometimes she fancied she caught a gleam of sympathy in her mother's soft, dark eyes, but it offered little hope. Mrs. Ito held her husband up as head of the house. She would not feel it proper to interfere, even for the sake of her daughter's happiness.

Shina had never felt more alone, or more like a wishbone. She shared her feelings with Kevin when he came that night.

"Why don't we simply elope?" she burst out. "Once we are married, Father will have to accept it." The unspoken words *and you* hung heavy in the quiet apartment.

Longing sprang to Kevin's eyes. Determination quickly replaced it.

"Don't tempt me, Shina," he huskily told her. A strong hand smoothed her already shining cap of dark hair. "I want nothing more than to marry you, but I won't do it behind your father's back." A thread of steel pushed into his voice. "I pray he will change. If he does not and we both feel it is God's will, we may one day marry without his blessing, but it will not be without his knowledge."

"You're right," she whispered. A little later, they knelt, joined hands, and recommitted themselves to finding and doing God's will. After Kevin left, Shina relived the proud moment when he refused to even consider her suggestion. In his own way, Kevin could be as stubborn as her father. Her eyes rounded. She took a quick breath. Was that part of the reason she loved him so much?

Shina pondered the thought. Yet her last conscious thoughts were not of her beloved, but of Nancy. Her friend's face shimmered in the night, especially the luminous look in Nancy's eyes when Shina shared the message of hope.

The tiny nurse stirred, whispered a prayer for the Bartons, then dropped into a deep and untroubled sleep.

fourteen

A few miles away from Shepherd of Love Hospital, Nancy Barton opened her eyes. She glanced at the digital clock on the nightstand. Bright red numerals proclaimed to the world it was 2:30 a.m.

What had awakened her? Not Damon. His even breathing beside her showed how deeply he slept. A wave of tenderness passed through her for the tall doctor who had captured her heart. She not only loved Damon, she respected him with all her heart. Unwilling to disturb him when she knew how weary he must be, she refrained from moving closer.

A feeling of unease brushed feathery fingers against reason. *Why?* Nancy thought of the hours since she left Shina. She and Damon had found nothing but friendliness in the community church a few blocks away. Predominantly Caucasian, those who attended obviously cared more about Christ than skin color. The Bartons thoroughly enjoyed the rousing hymn sing, prayers, and testimonies from the twenty or so persons present.

"A real old-fashioned prayer service," Damon had said in satisfaction on the way home. "You don't find many of them now." He swung Nancy's hand. "Too bad. I agree with a minister friend of mine who maintains 'so goes the prayer meeting, so goes the church.' "

"So do I." Nancy squeezed his fingers and inhaled flower-scented air. "I'm glad we're close enough to walk when it's nice. Summer, daylight saving time, and the many street lights give a feeling of security, don't they?"

The rest of the evening had gone just as smoothly. *So why do I feel something is terribly wrong?* Nancy wondered. She

148

stiffened at the heartless wail of a distant siren and didn't relax until its mournful echo lessened and died. The clock numerals said 4:00 before her weary body forced her to sleep.

Nancy groggily awakened to the fragrance of orange juice and hot chocolate. A glance at the clock showed she had overslept and needed to hurry. She snatched a light robe, ran downstairs, and followed her nose to the kitchen.

"Why didn't you shake me? I slept right through the alarm!"

Fresh-shaven and immaculate in a light summer suit, Damon smiled at her tousled hair and lipstick-free mouth.

"Actually, I shut it off before it buzzed. You looked too peaceful to disturb." The toaster pushed up delicately browned bread. "You have plenty of time. I fixed breakfast."

"My goodness, two meals in a row? At this rate, I'll be spoiled rotten."

A poignant light brightened his dark eyes. "Nothing on earth could ever spoil you rotten, Nancy." He cleared his throat. "Can't say the same for this toast, if we don't hurry up and eat it."

On a note of laughter and love, they finished breakfast and he drove her to Shepherd of Love. Nancy felt surrounded by a warm, soapsuds bubble when she watched him drive away. It burst into unpleasant, staining dampness the second she stepped inside the hospital doors. Patti Thompson and Shina Ito nabbed her on the way to Pediatrics. Their sober faces warned something was amiss even before Patti said, "You've read the paper, I suppose."

"We haven't started it at our new place. What's wrong?" Nancy asked. A premonition of trouble beat against her mind.

Tears of helplessness and rage filled Patti's expressive blue eyes.

"Last night, I mean early this morning, someone set fire to a church a few miles from here."

Nancy felt as if a giant hand had gripped her throat and

shut off the power of speech. She finally gasped, "Which one?" A preposterous idea brought cold sweat. It crawled down Nancy's back inside her peach uniform tunic. What if. . .no, it couldn't be! Not the friendly neighborhood community church whose parishioners had welcomed Damon and her so warmly the night before!

"It's the large Baptist church on the corner of—" Shina named streets. Her understanding glance steadied Nancy, but the rose-pink lips that matched Shina's uniform trembled. "The paper says it's definitely arson and racially motivated. Almost the entire congregation is African American."

"How can anyone be so wicked?" Patti sobbed. She grabbed Nancy in a fierce hug, muttered, "Excuse me. I have to wash my face," and ran down the corridor.

Shina glanced both ways to see they were not being observed. She bent close to Nancy and said in a low voice, "This isn't against you personally, you know. There have been other African-American church burnings in Seattle since those first arson attacks in the south and back east." She swallowed hard. "Remember the message." She shook her friend's nerveless arm and softly quoted, "'One day, the glowing embers of hatred that spawns persecution will be stamped out. . . .' Hang in there, Nancy."

Nancy's frozen state changed to pulsing life. "I will," she promised. She matched her stride to Shina's shorter steps and the two nurses headed toward their mercifully demanding jobs. At least for a time, there would be little opportunity to brood.

"Dr. Barton wants you to call him right away," Susan Devers told Nancy when she reached Pediatrics.

"So soon? He must have heard news of the church burning on the car radio and called from the cell phone," the younger nurse murmured.

Her LPN's reaction matched Patti Thompson's.

"I'd like to lock up whoever is responsible and bury the

key," Susan grumbled. The belligerence in her face showed she meant every word.

Woe unto any troublemaker who crossed paths with Susan Devers when she was in this mood, Nancy irrelevantly thought. It brought a smile to her own face.

"So do a lot of others, me included In the meantime, our patients wait." Nancy gestured toward the children, faces trustingly turned toward those who cared for them. If only those children and countless others like them could grow up in a world free of hatred and prejudice!

"Nurth Nanthy, I have a looth tooth," a grinning urchin called. He obligingly wiggled it with a stubby finger.

"So you do! My, it's almost ready to come out, isn't it?" Nancy said admiringly. Her day's work had begun, but first she must return Damon's call. He would be at the office by now. She slowly punched in the numbers. A few moments later she cradled the phone, warmed by Damon's concern. He had only wanted to make sure she was all right.

Nancy turned to her duties. Jason's eager smile made her heart ache. Even the understanding policies of Shepherd of Love could not stretch to keep a child who needed nothing but a home. She bit her lip, hugged the little boy as she had each of the others, and passionately wished she were in a position to adopt Jason.

❧

Early in the morning following the day Curtis Barton found the Lord in a nondescript motel room, he called Stone from the cell phone he'd installed in his car after the Idaho incident. It was unlikely the motel phone was bugged, but he'd take no chances. Neither would he show up at Stone's office at this critical stage of the "cat and mouse" game being played out. White supremacists openly boasted of their ability to infiltrate any organization, any level of government. No sense taking chances.

"Stone? Sorry, but we mislaid your order for flowers and

didn't get them delivered yesterday. We'll get on it this morning, okay?"

Cold, dead silence greeted his carefully guarded message. Curtis could almost hear the wheels of the agent's keen mind begin to turn. At last Stone grunted and said, "See that you do. I can't stand slipshod service." *Bang!* went the phone.

What a relief! The curt reply showed Stone had received the message loud and clear, and that he approved of Curtis's return to his florist delivery job.

After a quick shower and breakfast, Curtis knelt by the bed. This praying thing was new to him. He knew no fancy phrases, no formal prayers. Yet he wanted to talk to God.

"Thanks, God," he said huskily. "I guess if You care enough about a guy like me to send Your Son, You'll show me what I'm supposed to do now."

He waited, felt the same peace that had entered his heart the day before, and rose comforted. Would the florist see a change in him? He hoped so. If only he could tell Damon and Nancy the wonderful thing that had come into his life!

"Not safe to call, but I can send a telegram," Curtis muttered. He scribbled and rejected a dozen messages. What-ever he sent must be innocent enough not to arouse suspicion should it fall into the wrong hands.

His gaze turned to the Gideon Bible. A small smile curved his lips until he looked more like his brother than ever.

"I'll just bet I can find something in here to let Damon know his prodigal brother has—that's it!"

He chuckled and turned pages until he came to the story of the lost son. Choosing verses to best convey his change of heart, Curtis copied down *Luke 15171824*. A short time later, he repeated them to a puzzled employee in a local copy shop, paid his fee, and whistled his way to work.

"What did you do, win the lottery?" a coworker demanded while they loaded flowers for delivery. "You haven't stopped grinning since we got here."

Curtis felt his mouth stretch even wider. "Just made a new Friend."

"So? Everyone has friends."

"Not like this one." Curtis felt a thrill go through him.

"How come?"

"He died so I could live."

A look of alarm crossed the inquisitive worker's face. He hastily stepped backward.

"Whadd'ya you mean by that? Hey, man, are you some kind of murderer, or something?"

"No way! Just a sinner who finally had the guts to admit it," Curtis cheerfully said. "My new Friend's name is Jesus. I'll tell you about Him sometime, if you like." He swung into the driver's seat of the flower van and drove away, laughing at the blank expression on the other's face. Speaking of his new Friend hadn't been all that hard.

If it weren't for the continuing threat of danger, and being under orders not to contact Damon and Nancy, Curtis would have been happier than he had been since childhood days with his mother and brother. He found a Christian music station on the van radio and played it constantly. Now and then a long-forgotten hymn stirred a chord of memory. He found himself remembering a few words and singing along. He also bought a Bible and a marking pen. He painstakingly highlighted the same verses in his new possession that someone once marked in the motel Bible. Later he would read the whole Book. For now, it was enough just to study the words that made the path to salvation clear.

News of the burning of the African-American church touched Curtis deeply. A few weeks earlier he would have raged and planned revenge against whoever torched the church. Now he trembled at the terrible position in which those responsible had placed themselves. Not just in the eyes of the law, but in the eyes of God. Sweat broke out on his forehead. Never had he burned a church, yet he had done other things equally abhorrent. Thank God for His miraculous forgiveness through Jesus Christ!

Curtis awoke in the dark hours of the morning from a dream so vivid he leapt from bed. He'd been delivering bouquets and plants late the night before and had been exhausted. Now he dressed. An urgency he had never before experienced drove him to the dark sedan that blended well with the night. Compelled against reason, he drove the city streets until he came within a few blocks of the recently-burned church. He parked, killed the motor, stuffed his cell phone into his back pocket, and walked to the site. The acrid stench of blackened timbers filled his nostrils. The taste of fear turned his mouth metallic.

Why was he here? Why did he automatically stop in a tree-shadowed spot that permitted no ray from nearby street lights? What did he expect to find? Certainly not the deserted scene that duplicated what he'd seen on the evening news. He stared at the dimly lit skeleton of what had once been a house of worship.

A nagging feeling of something wrong became an obsession. Curtis rubbed his eyes. Truth struck like a flaming arrow. What he saw was not the TV image, but the one from his dream. A figure crept from behind the ruin, straight toward Curtis in his frail cover.

Curtis crouched lower, his muscles taut.

The figure paused, straightened. It flung back its head until the street light shone directly on a man's face. He laughed in a low, jeering tone, raised a baseball cap from close-cropped hair, doffed it toward the remains of the church, and swept a mocking bow. Curtis was close enough to catch the man's quiet taunt, "Prettiest fire I ever set, except one." A string of curses followed.

Excitement flowed through Curtis. He bit the inside of his mouth to keep from crying out. *Auger-Eyes!* The figure who gloated over the desolate sight was the convicted felon and active local hate group member, Emil Schwartz-Marshall-Elliott-Smith.

He must not get away. The thought beat in Curtis' head like a gong. Schwartz could only be stopped if taken by surprise. Such men went armed. A single false move could easily bring death to an attacker. Curtis set his jaw. So be it. Death held no fear since he had met the Master. Schwartz must be captured, no matter at what cost. Evil could not be allowed to continue.

Muscles turned to steel by months tramping through the rugged Idaho mountains tensed. Curtis waited, like a mountain lion ready to spring on unsuspecting prey. Nearer and nearer came the enemy. *Now.*

Had a voice spoken? Curtis obeyed without knowing. He launched himself like a silent missile. He wrapped iron-strong arms around the unsuspecting arsonist's body and felled him before Schwartz could collect his wits and reach for his piece. A dull thud followed. Schwartz went limp. *Had he hit his head?* Curtis wondered. Exploring fingers came away sticky. They confirmed Curtis's suspicions. Schwartz had knocked himself out on the pavement. His breathing was regular but he gave no sign of returning to consciousness.

"Thanks, God." Curtis panted for breath and considered his options. Should he take his prisoner to the nearest police station? No, better try to contact Stone. He found a handkerchief in Schwartz's pocket, folded it into a pad, and pressed it to his prisoner's forehead. Soon the bleeding dwindled to a seep.

What if he couldn't get Stone this early? Curtis grinned and pulled out his cell phone. Unlikely. From what he could tell, the FBI man was a machine, so intent on apprehending criminals and stopping violence he neither ate, slept, nor lived outside his office! A person had to admire a guy like that.

"Stone," the agent answered.

"Anthony Homeport. Steak: well done, $19.95." Curtis informed him. Would the agent correctly translate the message to: Schwartz, stakeout, fire at 1995, address of the recently burned church?

Stone's reply, "Be there with bells on" would mean nothing to a possible spy. It conveyed full understanding to Curtis, along with an ominous note in the gravely voice that warned Mr. Amateur Detective Barton he was in for the grandfather of all chew outs.

Schwartz continued to lie as one dead. Stone arrived alone, checked Schwartz, and listened to Curtis's story before summoning an ambulance. In the interminable time before it arrived, the agent's gaze turned sharp enough to cut solid marble. "Just can't keep from playing the hero, can you?" he barked. Sarcasm dripped from every syllable.

"I'm no hero. You won't believe me, but I woke from a dream so real I felt compelled to come here. I had no idea why until I recognized Schwartz."

"You what?" Stone's jaw dropped, the first sign of shock the younger man had ever seen him show. "Are you in the habit of running around in the middle of the night because of dreams?" He sounded incredulous.

Curtis felt drained. "No. It never happened before."

"By all that's holy, it had better not happen again," Stone began. The sound of an ambulance siren mercifully cut short whatever less-than-elegant words he'd planned to use on Curtis. Stone ordered, "Get out of here. Now. I'll get in touch later." He scowled ferociously. "You didn't forget anything, did you?"

"No, but something's bothering me." Curtis tried to focus his befuddled brain. "When Schwartz said this was the prettiest fire he had ever set, he added, 'except one.' Has he been arrested or convicted for arson?"

"Naw." Stone's eyes gleamed. "I wonder what he meant by that."

A suspicion too horrible to voice dried Curtis's throat to a crisp. "You don't think—Damon and Nancy?" *Please, God, no*, his heart silently shouted.

"We'll find out," Stone grimly said. "Leave your car. Get in mine, but stay out of sight. That's an order."

He shoved Curtis toward an unmarked car. Nothing distinguished it from hundreds of others that daily traveled Seattle streets.

Curtis numbly stepped into the passenger seat and hunkered down. An eternity later an ambulance and two police cars arrived. A second eternity passed, then Stone slid behind the wheel.

"They aren't taking him to Shepherd of Love, I hope," Curtis mumbled.

"Think I'm stupid? I don't bed down wounded wolves in a pen of lambs." Stone started the motor. "Until I tell you otherwise, you weren't here tonight. Schwartz won't know who attacked him." He smiled like a cat who just finished eating a sour mouse. "Maybe we'll get lucky and he never will. He got a pretty good crack on the head."

A chill went through Curtis. "Don't you believe what I told you?"

"Sure." Stone looked surprised. "Getting out of bed and heading for a burned-out church because you had a dream and strange feeling is too farfetched—even for you—to be anything but true!"

Curtis couldn't have held back his bellow of laughter if his life had depended on it. It exploded into the car and brought a wry smile to Stone's wintry lips.

The next instant it died, leaving Curtis dreading what they might find at the end of their journey. Just a few miles but it felt longer than around the world.

"This is the street," Stone announced a lifetime later. He turned a corner. "Well, we know what Schwartz's 'except one' meant."

Curtis could only stare in horror. Not at a church this time. Not at the Bartons' beloved new home. Instead, the remainder of a huge blackened cross marred the yard. It dripped streams of foam. Sympathetic-looking firemen busily gathered their equipment, faces averted.

Forgetful of the need to keep away, Curtis burst from the car with Stone right behind him.

"Damon?" he shouted through the noise of the gathered spectators.

"Here."

The pathos in the answer tore at Curtis's heart. He and Stone elbowed their way through the crowd to where Damon stood with his arm around Nancy.

"Thank God you're all right!" He caught Damon's shoulders with strong hands.

"All right!" Nancy choked out. She looked like a terrified sleepwalker waking in a strange place. "How can we be all right when we're awakened by a rock hurled through our bedroom window? When we find a burning cross on our lawn like something in a historical movie?" A sob escaped.

Stone took charge.

"Go home," he ordered the gaping onlookers. "Now." A few muttered, but the crowd dispersed. "Dr. and Mrs. Barton, come inside, please. You, too." He nodded at Curtis. "Make coffee if you know how."

Over steaming cups, he quietly said, "Hang in there. Thanks to this brother of yours, we had a real breakthrough tonight. You know what they say. The good Lord protects fools and children." He quickly related events. "With all we have on Schwartz, I won't be surprised if he sings like a flock of canaries." A curious smile came to Stone's weatherbeaten face. "No, I won't be surprised at all."

fifteen

Somehow the Bartons made it through the nightmarish day. Before noon, Damon had the charred remains of the cross down and hauled away. A stop at a garden department produced sod for the scorched area in the smooth green lawn where the symbol of hatred had flamed.

Damon leaned on the rake and smiled at his wife. "Good as new."

"On the outside." Nancy felt her mouth quiver and hastily raised her chin.

"We're going to make it through," he told her, forehead wrinkled in concern.

"I know." She didn't add, *at least this time*. God had promised deliverance. He just hadn't said when it would come. She felt the same way early that evening when Damon called her to the window and said in an odd voice,

"Looks like Simmons is entertaining." Nancy silently watched as one by one, their new neighbors scuttled up the walk to the house next door. Some cast furtive glances at the Barton home. Others looked down, or straight ahead.

"I guess we're the only ones not invited," she said bitterly. "I'd say it's more likely a meeting. I can see it now, all these good people, shocked out of their complacency. Some, especially Simmons, will express outrage. Yet in the long run, they'll decide they have no choice. They'll send a delegation to appeal to us on behalf of the neighborhood."

She deepened her voice into mimicry of an embarrassed man.

"'Uh, Dr. and Mrs. Barton, we don't have anything against you. However, under the circumstances, we're sure you must see it's best for all concerned if you move.'"

Nancy's eyes stung. "I also predict from now on there will be a gentleman's agreement about whom homeowners will sell to when someone moves!"

Damon swung from the window, eyes blazing. The next moment, an expression of hopelessness sponged away his anger.

"Can we really blame them? They do seem to be good people, especially Simmons. They're also terrified. I saw the way they looked at the blazing monstrosity before the firefighters put it out. For years, this has been a peaceful place to live, an oasis of quiet in the middle of a frightening world. A good place to bring up kids." His face contorted. "That's why we chose it, remember?"

Nancy could only mutely nod, cut to the core by the pain in his face.

"We came," Damon went on in the same lifeless voice. "Suddenly, everything changed. Frightening incidents began to happen. Graffiti. Death warnings. A rock through our window. Now, a cross burning. How can they—or we—keep from wondering what will happen next? A drive-by shooting? One of the children caught in crossfire?" His voice shook. "Have you ever been in the woods and seen a mother bear spring to the defense of her cubs? Through no fault of ours, these people have been exposed to danger. Who can condemn them for taking whatever steps they feel necessary in order to fight back?"

"No matter what it does to us."

"No matter what it does to us." Damon turned back to the window and stared into the pleasant evening that held no beauty for the Bartons. His shoulders slumped.

"Maybe they're right. Do we have the right to stay, if it means endangering others?"

Nancy's rage dissolved. She unhappily admitted, "I've asked myself that a hundred times." She looked around the home she had learned to love so deeply, even in the short time they'd lived there. "It will break my heart to leave." The instant the words left her lips, Nancy knew she had bowed to the inevitable. So far no one had been hurt, but the attacks were becoming more and more sinister. She and Damon could not remain, if their presence meant inflicting violence on innocent persons.

Twenty minutes later the doorbell rang. Damon opened it to the delegation Nancy had predicted would approach them. She saw a muscle twitch in his cheek, the only sign of inner perturbation.

"Come in," he quietly told Simmons, Adams, a group of men, and a scattering of women on the Barton porch. Every family in the immediate vicinity had a representative. They crowded the hall. Damon ushered them into the living room and motioned them to be seated. He remained standing by the fireplace, one arm around Nancy. She glanced from face to unrevealing face. All her attempts to understand and forgive melted like snow in Snoqualmie Pass when warm weather came.

Simmons cleared his throat.

"Uh, Dr. Barton, Mrs. Barton, each time something comes up that affects the neighborhood, we have meetings to discuss problems. We had such a meeting tonight."

"We noticed."

Simmons ignored Damon's flat response.

"Sorry not to include you, but we felt you, uh, might not feel comfortable if you were present."

Comfortable? Nancy clutched her Christian principles with both hands to keep from screaming. *How dare these people enter my home, my living room, and profess to be concerned about mine and Damon's feelings?* She moved closer to him and waited for the death blow she knew would follow. *Why doesn't he beat them to the punch and tell this modern vigilante group we have already decided to vacate their precious home? Should I? No. Let them play out the farce.*

Simmons took a deep breath. "No sense beating around the bush. Most of us have lived here for years. The area's been amazingly free from crime. We want it to stay that way."

Damon's arm tightened on Nancy's shoulder but he said nothing.

Simmons shifted position. His good-natured face lost its friendly look.

"What's happening here has to be stopped. Now. No matter what it takes."

Nancy's lip curled. *Those were the exact words she had prophesied would be spoken. Now for the clincher, the we're-so-sorry-but-please-get-out speech.* Damon's fingers bit into her flesh until she flinched. She could feel the hard beat of his hurting heart.

Simmons stood. "As spokesman for the homeowners around here, I'll give it to you straight." His eyes flashed and he took an impulsive step forward. "This kind of thing will not be tolerated. We voted unanimously to stand behind you and do everything possible to prevent such a thing ever happening again."

Nancy gasped. Damon echoed it. His breathing quickened.

"You mean you aren't asking us to move?"

Simmons swore, apologized, and said, "Move? Not on your life!" His hand shot out and engulfed Damon's. "We were afraid you might think something of the kind when we didn't ask you to the meeting. It couldn't be helped. There had to be a time for everyone to speak."

Damon shook his head, as if dazed. Nancy put one hand over her heart to still its wild pounding. Steel bands holding her body rigid loosened. She let her gaze travel from face to face. *Had they changed, or was it her perception?* Many still held fear, but courage and steady determination also shone brightly.

"The way we see it, too many decent folks are running

scared and giving into gangs and the like," Simmons explained. "Each time makes it easier to happen somewhere else. Some people are starting to take back their neighborhoods. We don't aim to wait until it comes to that. By refusing to be intimidated and standing together, we're going to hang onto what we've got."

Nancy felt a great gushing inside. She blindly muttered, "Excuse me" and headed for the closest bathroom. When she came back red-eyed, but dry-eyed, a sympathetic murmur went through the crowd. Damon's meaningful look threatened to start the waterworks again. The security of those who cared wrapped around her like an electric blanket on the highest setting. Her voice sounded small when she timidly said, "Damon and I decided just tonight we didn't have the right to stay and put you in danger."

Adams exploded into speech. Nancy hadn't realized the ordinary-appearing man could be so eloquent.

"We're not asking you to stay just for your sake," he said. "It's for us, too. Like Simmons said, if we don't rear up on our hind legs and speak out, who's to say which one of us will be the next target?"

His mouth set in a grim slit. "I remember an old poem about a guy who looked the other way every time the hangman came for an innocent person. He reasoned it had nothing to do with him and ignored a whole lot of cries for help. One day the hangman came for him. He yelled for someone to come save him. There was no one left to hear."

A little murmur went through the crowd, but no one spoke until Simmons made a move toward the door.

"We've taken up enough of your time."

"I don't know how we can ever repay you. Any of you," Damon said huskily.

Simmons grinned at Damon, then Nancy. "Want us to send you a bill?"

The crowd swept out in the general laugh that followed.

Nancy knew her eyes shone like twin stars, reflecting the unexpected and priceless gift they had just received. Those same eyes clouded when the door closed behind their loquacious neighbor Simmons, last to exit.

"I misjudged them so badly," she choked out. "All the time I thought they were. . ."

Damon turned a shining gaze on her. "So did I. Thank God for them! I've never admired a group of persons more." He checked the outside doors to make sure they were locked, then arm-in-arm he and Nancy climbed the stairs together.

That night proved a turning point. Persecution ceased entirely. Damon and Nancy discussed it. Was the capture of Schwartz responsible or the citizen patrols that nightly walked the area? In any event, peace reigned. The Bartons' tired minds and bodies found rest. Their service to others continued.

Nancy began to secretly hope she could approach Damon about Jason, but reluctantly held off. The raveled ends of too many loose threads must be painstakingly tied before they could even consider such a serious step. Curtis was again incommunicado. At Stone's order? Probably. The FBI agent had also apparently vanished. He neither called nor came by. A day passed. Another. A week. Life went back to normal, broken only by a startling piece of news.

"Look!" An ecstatic Shina waylaid Nancy on her way to Pediatrics. Patti Thompson stood grinning just behind the tiny nurse. Shina held out her left hand. A sparkling golden band with a topaz set in small diamonds encircled Shina's third finger!

Nancy gasped. "When—how—I thought—"

Shina's face crumpled, bearing evidence of the strain she had been under.

"Father sent for Kevin and me just last night. He asked if we still wished to be married." Shina's lovely black eyes misted. "We told him yes, but that we had promised to abide by whatever God wanted in our lives. Father folded his hands and said, 'I have considered well everything you told me. I have prayed much, to learn what is right.' " A bright drop fell, splashing on the new and cherished ring.

Patti impatiently burst out, "Hurry and tell the rest, before I do!"

Shina swiped at her wet eyes. "Father asked us to kneel. He laid one hand on each of our heads and said, 'This is a good and honorable man, daughter. Your mother and I give you formal permission to marry. Go with our blessing.'"

She took a deep, tremulous breath. "It was like a wedding ceremony, although of course we'll be married here in the chapel." Her voice quivered. "Kevin and I know this is an answer to prayer, especially having Father include Mother in the giving of consent and blessing. Neither of us believes it would have happened if we hadn't come to the place where we looked past our own desires, for His."

"And so they lived happily ever after," the irrepressible Patti caroled. A look of dismay crossed her face. "Hey, why am I so happy? Jonica, Nancy, Lindsey, now Shina. I'm the only old maid nurse left around here!"

"What about that dashing pilot of yours?" Shina teased.

Patti pretended nonchalance. "Oh, yes." Her blue eyes danced. "Maybe I won't be left to wither on the vine after all." She glanced at her watch. "Oh-oh. Gotta run." She grinned and took off.

"I am so glad for you, Shina. I feel you will be as happy as I am with Damon. You deserve it. You're special." Nancy hugged the smaller nurse.

"Thanks, Nancy." Shina enthusiastically returned the hug. "When Kevin slipped the ring on my finger and kissed me, I felt things couldn't get any better. He is so tender, so loving." She solemnly looked into her friend's face. "Life will be absolutely perfect as soon as God takes care of your problems. I have the feeling it's going to happen soon."

"It can't be too soon for me." Nancy grimaced. "Everything's been so quiet this past week, it's like sitting on a ticking bomb, waiting for it to detonate."

"It may not happen that way," Shina told her. She patted Nancy's hand. "God has a way of doing the unexpected. This is evidence." She pointed to her ring, then hurried away to the mothers and babies she loved.

The time bomb stopped ticking so suddenly it felt anticlimactic. After the week of uneasy silence, Damon and Nancy arrived home one late afternoon to find Curtis and Stone waiting. Nancy's heart thudded to her feet, until the two men bounded from the cars parked in front of the Barton residence. One glance reassured her. Never in all the time the Bartons had known the FBI agent had he displayed the excitement even his poker face and angry eyes could not successfully hide. Or the broad grin that changed him from official to a highly likable human being.

"It's over!" Curtis yelled. He raised his arms to the summer sky and clasped them in a victory signal.

Stone's crustiness returned. "Wait until we're inside, can't you?"

"Yeah." Curtis didn't sound one bit repentant. He bounded up the steps and grinned at Nancy while Damon unlocked the door.

"What's been happening?" Damon inquired when the four were seated. He reached for Nancy's hand and her fingers curled into his palm.

Stone took charge.

"Like Curtis said, it's over." His eyes gleamed. "We've got us a nice little bunch of white supremacists in the slammer waiting to stand trial." He paused. "For murder." Satisfaction oozed in every word.

A shiver went through Nancy. Her ears roared. She forced herself to concentrate on what Stone was saying.

"I was right about our friend Emil Schwartz. He's a fringe lunatic, willing to do everything except murder. I played a hunch and told him we had an eyewitness to the murder in Idaho. Schwartz's eyes told me he knew exactly what I was talking about. He'd been there, even though he denied it. He caved in when I showed him the police sketch and told him he'd been recognized." Stone laughed outright, obviously enjoying himself.

"But Curtis didn't recognize him," Damon protested.

Stone looked the picture of aggrieved innocence. "No one said he did. I only said Schwartz had been recognized. He had, by you and Mrs. Barton. Is it my fault the creep's guilty conscience made him leap to the conclusion the second man in the mountains was the one who I.D.'d him?"

Curtis could remain silent no longer. "No way was Schwartz going to take the rap for a murder he didn't commit. He cut a deal."

Stone sent him a quelling glance. "Who's telling this story, anyway?" A twitch at the corner of his mouth showed sarcasm was more habit than annoyance.

"Did it take all week to make him talk?" Nancy asked in a small voice.

"No, but it took time for him to lead us to the trapper's grave under a pile of rocks not far from the deserted survival camp," Stone explained. "We had to wait for forensics to make a positive identification and to get the ballistics report. Schwartz tipped us off on the whereabouts of our quarry. In a surprise raid, we rounded up the men Schwartz fingered, including those who actually did the shooting." Some of his satisfaction vanished. "We'll never get all of them, worse luck, but the backbone of this particular hate group is broken." Stone stood. So did the others. The smile he gave Nancy was singularly sweet, more so because of its rare presence on his lined face. He yawned mightily. Nancy felt her own jaw muscles stretch in sympathy.

"I'm going home and sleep for a week. I suggest you two do the same," he told her and Damon.

"What about me?" Curtis complained.

"What about you? Now that this stinking mess is over, you might consider what you're going to do with the rest of your life," Stone snapped.

"If I didn't have a record, I might consider being an FBI agent like you." Curtis said meekly, but his eyes twinkled.

"Fat chance." Again Nancy had the feeling Stone didn't mean half of his gruffness. She believed it even more when Stone added with a gleam in his eye, "Besides, you'd have to learn to take directions. From what I've seen, that's not your strong suit. Why don't you go in business for yourself? That way, no one can tell you what to do. You'll eventually have the money, if you aren't too proud to take it. "He strode out without a good-bye or backward glance.

"What did he mean?" Damon asked after they sat down again.

Curtis looked troubled, but his dark gaze met his brother's head-on. "We need to talk about it." He fitted his fingers together. "Seems there was a large reward offered for information leading to the arrest and conviction of the leaders of this group. Stone's positive they will be convicted. He says the reward's mine. I don't think so." He looked appealingly from his brother to Nancy. "I'm no bounty hunter! Anyway, now that I've accepted Christ, how can I take it?"

"That's a tough one," Damon admitted. His fine forehead knitted in thought. "You certainly didn't report the murder with the idea of financial gain in mind."

"Of course not, but what's God going to think about my collecting a reward for helping send someone to Death Row? I can't do it!"

The germ of an idea crawled into Nancy's brain. She leaned forward, hands on her knees, and hesitantly said, "Curtis, what if you used the reward to bring good from evil? There are organizations dedicated to preventing the expansion of hatred and prejudice. With cuts in government spending, such services are curtailed for lack of funds. It may take months, even years, to get a conviction. Between now and then, you'll have time to decide."

Relief swept over Curtis' face. "Thanks, Nancy. I'll do that."

"What are you going to do in the meantime?" Damon asked when Curtis rose.

His brother looked sheepish. "Believe it or not, I really like delivering posies. I'm going to stick with it." His grin died. "For years I added to the misery in the world. Now, I get smiles and joy when I march up to a house or apartment carrying bouquets of flowers." He cleared his throat. "Unless or until God tells me different, I'll keep on with my florist job."

Damon wordlessly gripped his brother's hand. Nancy placed hers on top of the other two and said, "You're welcome here any time you can come, Curtis."

"I know."

Curtis reverted to his cocky manner and flashed the charming smile that too often got him what he wanted and often led him into trouble. Whistling, he loped to his car, sun warm on his dark face and white smile. Just before he stepped inside he called, "See you in church. Literally." A quick wave and he was gone, leaving happiness behind him.

Heart too full for words, Nancy turned to Damon. He opened his arms and gathered her into his embrace. Joy over the revelations of the day brought release. Somewhere at this moment, embers of hatred and prejudice still glowed. Yet God reigned supreme, in control of a world that mocked, ignored, and fought against Him. Secure in her husband's love, protected by God's promises, Nancy rested. The past was gone forever. Tomorrow with all its challenges and rewards lay shrouded in the mists of yet-to-be. She and Damon had today, to live, to love, to serve, and to thank God for His goodness.

epilogue

Thy word is a lamp unto my feet, and a light unto my path (Psalm 119:105)

A graceful brown finger traced the scripture neatly engraved on Seattle's Shepherd of Love hospital director's door. A warm smile curved Nancy Galbraith Barton's tender lips, lighting candles in her dark eyes. Her immaculate peach pants uniform lent a glow to her brown-velvet skin.

A small hand slipped into hers. A small voice said, "I'm here, Mother."

A deeper, richer voice added, "So am I."

Nancy looked from seven-year-old Jason Street Barton's adoring face to the tall frame of her beloved husband. How could any woman ask for more? She freed her hand, put a slender arm around each of them, and whispered, "I know, my darlings. And I am glad."

A Letter To Our Readers

Dear Reader:

In order that we might better contribute to your reading enjoyment, we would appreciate your taking a few minutes to respond to the following questions. When completed, please return to the following:

Rebecca Germany, Managing Editor
Heartsong Presents
P.O. Box 719
Uhrichsville, Ohio 44683

1. Did you enjoy reading *Glowing Embers?*
   ❑ Very much. I would like to see more books
      by this author!
   ❑ Moderately
      I would have enjoyed it more if _____

   _____

2. Are you a member of **Heartsong Presents**? ❑Yes ❑No
   If no, where did you purchase this book? _____

   _____

3. What influenced your decision to purchase this
   book? (Check those that apply.)

   ❑ Cover   ❑ Back cover copy

   ❑ Title   ❑ Friends

   ❑ Publicity   ❑ Other_____

4. How would you rate, on a scale from 1 (poor) to 5
   (superior), the cover design? _____

5. On a scale from 1 (poor) to 10 (superior), please rate the following elements.

___Heroine   ___Plot

___Hero   ___Inspirational theme

___Setting   ___Secondary characters

6. What settings would you like to see covered in **Heartsong Presents** books?_____

_____

_____

7. What are some inspirational themes you would like to see treated in future books?_____

_____

_____

8. Would you be interested in reading other **Heartsong Presents** titles?   ❑ Yes   ❑ No

9. Please check your age range:
   ❑ Under 18   ❑ 18-24   ❑ 25-34
   ❑ 35-45   ❑ 46-55   ❑ Over 55

10. How many hours per week do you read? _____

Name _____

Occupation _____

Address _____

City_____ State_____ Zip _____

Colleen L. Reece takes girls ages 9 to 15 on nail-biting adventures in the Nancy Drew style, but with a clear Christian message. Super sleuth Juli Scott and her savvy friends find love and excitement and learn that it always pays to have a sense of humor. The first two titles in this mystery series are not to be missed.

___*Mysterious Monday*—Julie refuses to believe her father was killed in the line of duty as a policeman. With the help of her new friend Shannon, Julie sets out to reopen the case.

___*Trouble on Tuesday*—Shannon has gotten caught up in fortune telling and an uncanny prediction. In spite of everything her friends try to do, only God can save her from this web of deception.

Send to: Heartsong Presents Reader's Service
P.O. Box 719
Uhrichsville, Ohio 44683

Please send me the titles checked above. I am enclosing **$2.97 each** (please add $1.00 to cover postage and handling per order. OH add 6.25% tax. NJ add 6% tax.). Send check or money order, no cash or C.O.D.s, please.

To place a credit card order, call 1-800-847-8270.

NAME _____

ADDRESS _____

CITY/STATE _____ ZIP _____

·······Heart♥ng·······

HEARTSONG PRESENTS *TITLES AVAILABLE NOW:*

(If ordering from this page, please remember to include it with the order form.)

·········· Presents ··········

Great Inspirational Romance at a Great Price!

Heartsong Presents books are inspirational romances in contemporary and historical settings, designed to give you an enjoyable, spirit-lifting reading experience. You can choose wonderfully written titles from some of today's best authors like Veda Boyd Jones, Yvonne Lehman, Tracie J. Peterson, Nancy N. Rue, and many others.

When ordering quantities less than twelve, above titles are $2.95 each. Not all titles may be available at time of order.

Heartsong Presents
Love Stories Are Rated G!

That's for godly, gratifying, and of course, great! If you love a thrilling love story, but don't appreciate the sordidness of some popular paperback romances, **Heartsong Presents** is for you. In fact, **Heartsong Presents** is the *only inspirational romance book club*, the only one featuring love stories where Christian faith is the primary ingredient in a marriage relationship.

Sign up today to receive your first set of four, never before published Christian romances. Send no money now; you will receive a bill with the first shipment. You may cancel at any time without obligation, and if you aren't completely satisfied with any selection, you may return the books for an immediate refund!

Imagine. . .four new romances every four weeks—two historical, two contemporary—with men and women like you who long to meet the one God has chosen as the love of their lives. . .all for the low price of $9.97 postpaid.

To join, simply complete the coupon below and mail to the address provided. **Heartsong Presents** romances are rated G for another reason: They'll arrive *Godspeed!*